EX LIBRIS

VINTAGE **CLASSICS**

JANICE GALLOWAY

Janice Galloway's first novel, *The Trick is to Keep Breathing,* now widely regarded as a Scottish contemporary classic, was published in 1989 and won the MIND/Allan Lane Book of the Year. Her second novel, *Foreign Parts,* won the American Academy of Arts and Letters E. M. Forster Award while her third, *Clara,* about the tempestuous life of nineteenth-century pianist Clara Wieck Schumann, won the Saltire Award in 2002. Collaborative texts include an opera with Sally Beamish and three cross-discipline works with Anne Bevan, the Orcadian sculptor. Her 'anti-memoir', *This Is Not About Me,* was published by Granta in September 2008 to universal critical acclaim. Its successor, *All Made Up,* (a 'true novel'), also published by Granta, won Scottish Book of the Year 2012. Her latest book, *Jellyfish,* is a collection of stories published in 2015.

ALSO BY JANICE GALLOWAY

Fiction

Foreign Parts

Clara

Stories

Blood

Where You Find It

Collected Stories

Jellyfish

Memoir

This is Not About Me

All Made Up

JANICE GALLOWAY

The Trick
is to
Keep Breathing

VINTAGE

11

Vintage
20 Vauxhall Bridge Road,
London SW1V 2SA

Vintage Classics is part of the Penguin Random House group of
companies whose addresses can be found at
global.penguinrandomhouse.com.

Copyright © Janice Galloway 1989

This edition reissued by Vintage in 2015
First published in Great Britain by Polygon in 1989

The original publication of this book was given a grant towards
publication by the Scottish Arts Council

www.vintage-books.co.uk

A CIP catalogue record for this book is
available from the British Library

ISBN 9781784870133

Printed and bound by Clays Ltd, Elcograf S.p.A.

Penguin Random House is committed to a sustainable future
for our business, our readers and our planet. This book is
made from Forest Stewardship Council® certified paper.

For Alison and Margaret and Drew

I can't remember the last week with any clarity.

I want to be able to remember it because it was the last time anything was in any way unremarkable. Eating and drinking routinely, sleeping when I wanted to. It would be nice to remember but I don't.

Now I remember everything all the time. You never know what you might need to recollect later, when the significance of the moment might appear. They never give you any warning.

They never give you any warning.

ooo

I watch myself from the corner of the room
sitting in the armchair, at the foot of the stairwell. A small
white moon shows over the fencing outside. No matter how
dark the room gets I can always see. It looks emptier when
I put the lights on so I don't do it if I can help it. Brightness
disagrees with me: it hurts my eyes, wastes electricity and
encourages moths, all sorts of things. I sit in the dark for a
number of reasons.

The curtains are too wee to close properly so the draught
from the attic filters right through to the chair and makes me
cold. Streetlight gets in and makes the furniture glow at the
edges, like bits of sunk ship rising out of the wash of green.
You notice it more with the TV off. The carpet is ancient
with a sort of Persian design. In the daytime it has red and
blue shapes in the centre and green lines weaving them
together like ivy. Now it looks like seaweed. The threadbare
bits are charcoal and there's a black patch. Liquid black.
Still wet. It seeps when I put my shoe near, bleeding at the
rim of leather, sucking at the sole. I rock my foot back and
forth in the wet till it skids and jerks my knee. A sharp kind
of pain. I get stiff sitting for ages: my knuckles rust.
Clutching at the armrests as though I'm scared I'll fall. I
can't think where I've left my watch.

The green numbers on the stereo flash 03.25. But it goes fast.
I know perfectly well it doesn't matter what the real time is.
This is all beside the point. The fact remains it's so late it's
early and I have to move. I have to go upstairs. I have work
tomorrow and I have to go upstairs.

I look at the ceiling where upstairs is, then back at my hands.

I have to concentrate: one finger at a time, releasing pressure and rebalancing in the chair to accommodate the tilting, adjusting, redistributing pieces of myself. Hands are bastards: so many separate pieces. The muscles in the thighs tightening as the feet push down and the stomach clenching to take the weight then I'm out the chair, shaky but upright. My knees ache. I move, ignoring the carpet as it tries to nudge through the soles.

Square window on the landing, flat royal blue. Shadows of trees on the wall. It's always a good idea to stop here, looking up at the window before you start on the stairs; steady yourself and work out tactics. Sometimes I get the notion I have to take the stairs in one or something terrible might happen. Other times I take them one at a time and count, making sure they're all still there. Tonight, there's nothing. I haul up with the handrail for a rope and get filthy from the upstairs skirting. Strings of oose shelter in corners, waving ghost arms. It's time I got this place clean.

Five doors radiate from the top of the landing and every door is closed. I'm meticulous about the doors because of the noise they make when the wind rises, rattling and tapping on the wood surround. They knock. Also there's a mirror in the bathroom that's best avoided. I go straight to the bedroom, kicking off shoes despite the fact that it's freezing - you can't sleep in your shoes - then slice between the quilt and the mattress, making myself flat like cardboard. I read in a magazine once that to get warmer, you shouldn't curl into yourself but lie out full to spread the heat. I look out of the window, checking for a change in the sky, then close the curtain, reaching out with one stiff arm. I listen for the birds to come outside on the ledge. It always takes a long time.

*His finger traces the length of my spine before his
shadow lengthens, falls on one side of the towel.
The voice is overhead, far away.*

I'm going to swim.

*I go on lying flat, face buried in his shirt, listening
to bare feet receding on the tile. A faint slicking
noise of water; a heavy scent of oil and flowers.*

I get hotter.

*Tightness on my naked shoulders. I should be
careful of burning. The watch on the corner of
the towel says almost noon. Fifteen minutes. I am
sticking to the blue loops. They make marks on
my stomach.*

*I peel away from the towel, turn as I stand. The
pool is very bright in the sun. Disconnected limbs
come through the whiteness, the cries of children:
ripples slither along the surface.*

I am vaguely uneasy. Shivering.

I'm sticky. The black sleeve of my jacket reaching for the radio is furry with white from the covers. I've been dozing in my clothes. Outside, it's overcast but not raining. Leaves are cramping the drain and there's movement in the gutters. I reach for the radio and go downstairs. It takes the water half an hour to warm.

Thursday Morning.
Mornings are for function washes, not a full ritual. While the tap runs I strip at the top of the landing, putting the things I've slept in straight into the basket. This saves effort. Also I don't like to touch them again after I'm clean. I collect a towel and kneel in the bath. Sitting wastes time.

Hello.
The mirror behind the tap that shows a kneeling torso, head chopped off sheer at the white plastic rim. I put the mirror there because I couldn't work out how to hang it up without knocking lumps in the wall. Now I like it there: like looking through a window at someone else. Nipped in waist and pale, tight thighs with a pink scar where I was scalded a long time ago. The scar only shows when I wash but it's there all the time: waiting to surface through the skin when I hit the water, like invisible ink. Not so visible when it's luke-warm though. I splash to get used to the temperature then raise my arms and count the ribs. The mirror breasts tilt, nipples creasing in the draught from under the door. Then I wash. Just the soap and my hands taking the sweat of the night away. Making me sweet.

By the time I go downstairs, I'm au fait with the farming news, current value of the dollar and the yen, state of the roads in East Anglia, weather in Humber, Fisher, German Bight. There are interviews with junior ministers while I make tea. Always tea in the morning unless I've eaten the night before: then, it's black coffee. Bad mornings, I have only hot water. But I drink something, as much as I can. It helps the headache and the dryness: the weight of fluid is calming. I'm leaning back on the worktop with the cup between my hands when a note twitches on the lino.

PHONE DR. STEAD

Could be an old one: it's hard to tell. I check the clock and worry in case it's stopped. Sometimes I have to haul it off the wall and listen for the tick to be absolutely sure. It's OK. It's always OK: just a matter of waiting. I get nervous waiting. When I'm ready, I rinse the cup, mop the sink dry and lift my coat. My mouth is still dry as I lock the back door. My mouth is always dry.

ooo

Thursday 9.05.
The main door is cluttered with litter already and the sign is squint.

VISITORS MUST REPORT TO THE OFFICE

The office is open and nobody looks up. All the lights are on downstairs because the corridors are dark all day. They smell of hospital: later they will smell of gymnasium. As you go upstairs you pass a painting of some kind of fantasy domestic scene: a whole house painted in poster colours with mummy in the kitchen and dad in the garage while a variety of offspring lie in bed or watch tv or play on a snake-green lawn.

Marianne thought it would be difficult to go back. It was and it wasn't. Not what she thought. Work is not a problem. This is my workplace.
This is where I earn my definition, the place that tells me what I am.

11

Work is not a problem. I work in a school.
I teach children.
I teach them :

1. routine
2. when to keep their mouths shut
3. how to put up with boredom and
   unfairness
4. how to sublimate anger politely
5. not to go into teaching

That isn't true. And then again, it is. I am never sure what it is I do.

Shoulderbag, notepad, pieces of chalk. I check the timetable to make sure I have the right day. When the kids arrive I'm ready. I devise programmes and plan lessons, I lecture and consult and advise, talk too fast to follow and wave my arms like a windmill. They break sweat trying to keep up. I wind up like a clockwork mouse, eliciting response, raging to make a difference. Stasis scares me: I go stiff when I stop. So I pretend like hell and teach like a demon.

This is my workplace.
It tells me what I am.
I like to be good at what I am.

The nice thing is that I need not be present when I am working. I can be outside myself, watching from the corner of the room. Getting to work is a problem, handling mealtimes is a problem. But not the job. Something always attends to that. Kids like me. I am only the drama teacher and not a real threat. I let them wear make-up and play. Today there will be improvisations and trust exercises, silence games. No, work is not a problem. It never has been.

I am the problem.

The women are waiting in the car. We have this rapport: I

always sit in the back, always the same side and they never say much. They are aware they are doing me a favour and so am I. It's still not clear in my mind or theirs if I should offer them money for petrol or what. It's so easy to offend people. I only know I've done it when they draw looks. I look right back because I don't know any better and because my reflexes are slow these days: it goes with the dry mouth. Tonight one of them says she's going to see Fatal Attraction then we can all relax. Eventually, silently, we reach the bus stop. Their lipstick flashes through the grimy windows as they drive off together and I wait for the bus to take me to the next bus stop.

It takes two buses to get to where I have to go.

ooo

On the map, it's called Bourtreehill, after the elder tree, the bourtree, Judas tree; protection against witches. The people who live here call it Boot Hill. Boot Hill is a new estate well outside the town it claims to be part of. There was a rumour when they started building the place that it was meant for undesirables: difficult tenants from other places, shunters, overspill from Glasgow. That's why it's so far away from everything. Like most rumours, it's partly true. Boot Hill is full of tiny, twisty roads, wild currant bushes to represent the great outdoors, pubs with plastic beer glasses and kids. The twisty roads are there to prevent the kids being run over. The roads are meant to make drivers slow down so they get the chance to see and stop in time. This is a dual misfunction. Hardly anyone has a car. If one does appear on the horizon, the kids use the bends to play chicken, deliberately lying low and leaping out at the last minute for fun. The roads end up more conducive to child death than if they had been straight. What they do achieve is to make the buses go slow. Buses are infrequent so the shelters are covered in graffiti and kids hanging from the roofs. Nobody waits in these shelters even when it's raining. It rains a lot. The buses take a long time.

When I was small I always wanted a red front door. This front door is bottle green. The key never surrenders first time. I have to rummage through my bag and every pocket while I stand at the door as though I'm begging to be mugged. The first time we came, there were two sets of numbers on the door; one large and black; the other brass and much smaller. Like this:

13   13

We laughed and left them on, wondering if the previous tenants had been amnesiacs or phobics. When I came back alone, I took both sets off. There are four little holes on the door where they used to be

.

          .   :

and a different colour of paint underneath. I wondered what had moved away the previous tenants with their amnesia or their phobia. I wondered where they were now. Anyway, I didn't want those numbers on the door: it was a signal I could do without. I was angry I hadn't done it before. The nameplate was something he had bought, so I left it on. It says his name. Not mine.

Grit wells up when I open the door. There are always withered leaves in the porch. It seems to sit at the end of a natural tunnel of wind and makes itself difficult even on mild days. Litter accumulates on either side of the porch step: the porch is full of curled, brown leaves. Slaters run frantic in the sudden emptiness overhead while I fight my way inside. This makes me shiver. Every time. I notice a little shell of something dead that's been there for weeks now because I can't pick it up, not even through paper. I hate the feel of them, gritty little packets. Insects make me sick. They

14

have their skeletons outside, too many eyes, unpredictable legs and you can never tell where their mouths are. Spiders are worse. But today there are only the slaters. They disgust me but I'm not afraid of them. I push the letters with my foot till they are well clear of the dead one and pick them up with the tips of my fingers.

A bill from the lawyer, a note from the Health Visitor and a postcard from Marianne.

I've been Whitewater Rafting

The postcard has a picture of a butterfly and a gushing torrent of water in the background. The words on the back are smudged as though some of the water from the front of the card has splashed over and made the ink run. This makes it hard to read but I get the general drift.

Camping better than anticipated. Leaving for the
Canadian border tomorrow. Scenery wonderful.
You would hate it. Love   Mxx

I forget about the slaters and try to feel the other continent through the card. It doesn't work. I make tea and check out the livingroom. The spill on the rug is almost dry. I find the bottle open from last night but not the lid. I put an envelope over the neck, sitting the bottle aside so I don't kick it later, then reshape cushions trying to keep my feet on the rug because my shoes make a terrible noise on the floorboards. But things have to be set in place. A lot depends on stillness later and I have to get a lot of moving around out of my system now. Stillness helps when I'm alone. It keeps me contained.

Marianne and I talked a lot about what it would be like. I wanted an idea. We thought it was just a matter of getting by and letting time pass. Things would get better if I sat it out, just waiting, crossing off days. We talked about it, driving round in her car the evening before she left. I said What will I do while I'm lasting, Marianne? What will I do?

Tonight I have lots of choices:

15

three soaps
four comedy shows
four game shows
one blockbuster serial
two disaster movies
one western
two chat shows
one wildlife documentary
two socio-political documentaries
six sets of news in varying lengths
three sports slots
one investigation into the paranormal
one religious broadcast

The paranormal effort is at eleven thirty.
I wait while it gets dark, trying to get out of my own skin and
reach the corner of the room.

*I look out over the water, my hand to my eyes like
a sailor in a picture book. My lips draw back from
peering at the whiteness, the reflection of sun on the
pool. Shivering.*

Something catches my eye.

A red beachball.
Men slicking back wet hair.

*There are men at the side of the pool. They stand in
a rough O near the water, looking down. I am aware
of staring and try hard to smile in case people are
looking at me, then I swivel my head the length of
the water and back, searching.*

A red beachball.

Children sit on the rim of tile.
But there is something inevitable about the centre,
the hollow of the ragged O. I turn to face it. The
water is very bright.

ooo

The kitchen is bright, even at this time in the morning.
Yellow walls and white woodwork. Inside the white cupboard, a big green box silts at the corners, leaving snuff trails
on the floor of the shelf. Family Size Economy Green Label
(Strong) Tea. I have no entitlement to a family-size box but
it cuts costs: I drink a lot of tea. There is powdered milk in
a plastic container shaped like a milkbottle and a white
cylinder of saccharine. The cupboard always smells of green
label even though there are plenty of other things in there.
I once made a list of them and memorised it, just to see if I
could. Two tins of soup, dehydrated potato, several jars of
beetroot, table jelly, powdered custard, pineapple chunks,
packet sauces (cheese and parsley) and the tea things. They
all smell of tea. This morning, there's a note as well
                HEALTH VISITOR 12.30
so I phone school and say I won't come. They never ask why:
they're used to it by now.

Friday Morning 10.23.
There's a lot to do before she comes but it's a set routine so
I don't need to think. It just uses my body and runs itself,

hands picking up the cloth and wiping taps after I rinse the emptied cup. I begin cleaning the house.

I can't stop getting frantic about the house being clean and tidy for people coming. I used to watch my mother when I was a teenager and think I'm never going to do that: it's so pointless. I'd tell her things I'd read in books, that my mind was going to be more important than the thickness of the dust on my mantlepiece and she'd zoom the hoover too close to my feet shouting SHIFT to drown me out. I thought I knew something. I looked down my nose at the windolene sheen of my mother's house and knew better while my mother revved the hoover in the background and told me I was a lazy bitch.

I clean the kitchen till my hands are swollen from cold water, red as ham. My knuckles scrape and go lilac till the kitchen looks like they do on TV and smells of synthetic lemons and wax. I worry about the livingroom. It never looks right. I try not to worry. I try to be grateful since it took me long enough to get here, haggling with tiny-minded Mr Dick from the Housing Authority. Every fourth house in this estate is empty. Kids break the windows and the council have to pay to repair and maintain them empty so the rents go up all the time. Every time the rent goes up more houses become empty, some overnight. But Mr Dick said there were diffi-culties in my getting tenancy. They have to make a fuss so you know who's boss. There were rent arrears. I wasn't liable but Mr Dick exlained if I paid them it might ease the aforementioned difficulties. I said I hadn't got the money.

Mr Dick looked me right in the eye.
    Try to be a little more co-operative. We're bending over backwards. You're not helping yourself, creating difficul-ties. Strictly speaking, we're under no obligation to house you at all, not when you were never registered as tenant. We needn't do anything at all, strictly speaking. There has to be a bit of give and take. We're bending over backwards you know, bending over backwards.
I said I was sorry about all the trouble they were having on

my account and appreciated how good they were being. But I didn't have any money. Surely they understood I had all sorts of debts and expenses at a time like this. Besides the place didn't have a dustbin. Did he expect me to pay for no dustbin?

Mr Dick made his eyes go very small.

There was certainly one there when Mr Fisher became resident, Miss Stone. Oh yes, there was certainly a dustbin on the premises.

His eyes almost disappeared.

I suggest you know more about the whereabouts of this dustbin than you say. And the washing line. Miss Stone.

I paid for the missing things and they gave me back the keys. I got the house.

It's too big really. There are four rooms. One is decorated as a bedroom and the others randomly. There isn't enough furniture to go round. The two armchairs are covered with sheeting. Dust puffs up from underneath when someone sits on them or if they move, really old chairs. The curtains don't meet and are blue. The shelves are his: something to do before we went on holiday. That's why they're not finished. They asked for a receipt to prove the shelves were new, then let me have the benefit of the doubt. His wife didn't want them anyway. The shelves are white, complete enough to house the record player, books, magazines and the phone. The pile of records are mostly his. The Bowie poster hides wine stains where I threw a glass at the wall. A wee accident.

I rearrange things, placing chairs over the bald patches of the rug, sweeping the boards. It never looks as good as I'd like.

By twenty past I'm running along the twisty road between the houses to the shop for biscuits. She likes biscuits. I get different ones each time hoping they are something else she will enjoy. I can't choose in a hurry. I can't be trusted with custard creams so deliberately don't get them. Chocolate digestives are too expensive. I wait for too long in the queue

19

while a confused little kid tries to bargain for his father's cigarettes with the wrong money, so I have to run back clutching fig rolls and iced coffees and nearly drop the milk. I get flustered at these times, but I know I'll manage if I try harder. These visits are good for me. Dr Stead sends this woman out of love. He insisted.

I said, I'm no use with strangers.

He said, But this is different. Health Visiors are trained to cope with that. He said she would know what to do; she would find me out and let me talk. *Make me* talk.

HAH

I'm putting on the kettle, still catching my breath when she comes in without knocking and frightens me. What if I had been saying things about her out loud? I tell her to sit in the livingroom so I can have time to think.

    Tray

           jug

                sweeteners

                        plates

                              cups and saucers

                                    another spoon

                                        christ

the biscuits

the biscuits

I burst the wrap scundlessly and make a tasteful arrangement. I polish her teaspoon on my cardigan band. No teapot. I make it in the cup, using the same bag twice, and take it through as though I've really made it in a pot and just poured it out. Some people are sniffy about tea-bags. It sloshes when I reach to push my hair back from falling in my eyes and I suddenly notice I am still wearing my slippers dammit.

Never mind. She smiles and says

         Well!

This is to make out the tea is a surprise though it isn't. She does it every time. We sit opposite each other because that's the way the chairs are. The chairs cough dust from under their sheets as she crosses her legs, thinking her way into the part. By the time she's ready to start I'm grinding my teeth back into the gum.

HEALTH VISITOR	So, how are you/how's life/ what's been happening/ anything interesting to tell me/ what's new?
PATIENT	Oh, fine/ nothing to speak of.

I stir the tea repeatedly. She picks a piece of fluff off her skirt.

HEALTH VISITOR	Work. How are things at work? Coping?
PATIENT	Fine. [Pause] I have trouble getting in on time, but getting better.

I throw her a little difficulty every so often so she feels I'm telling her the truth. I figure this will get rid of her quicker.

HEALTH VISITOR	[Intensifying] But what about the day-to-day? How are you coping?
PATIENT	OK. [Brave smile] I manage.
HEALTH VISITOR	The house is looking fine.
PATIENT	Thank-you. I do my best.

This is overdone. She flicks her eyes up to see and I lower mine. She reaches for a biscuit.

HEALTH VISITOR	These look nice. I like a biscuit with a cup of tea.

We improvise about the biscuits for a while, her hat sliding back as she chews. She doesn't like the tea. Maybe she eats so many biscuits just to get rid of the taste.

HEALTH VISITOR	Aren't you having one? They're very good.
PATIENT	No, thanks. Maybe later. Having lunch soon.

She goes on munching, knowing I don't want her to be here/ that I do want her to be here but I can't talk to her.

This is the fourth time we have played this fucking game.

The first time was worst. I went through the tea ceremony for five minutes then tried to get the thing opened up.

What are supposed to come here for? I said.
She just looked.
What's it for? What are we supposed to talk about?
She said, I'm here to help you. To help you try to get better. I'm here to listen.
But I don't know you from a hole in the wall. I can't do it.
She said, You can tell me anything you like. I assure you it goes no further and I've heard it all before.

I could hear my own breathing. I knew Dr Stead was doing his best for me and that was why she was here. I had to try. It was reasonable. I swallowed hard. I can't remember what I said now. Whatever it was, I was in mid-flow, keeping my eyes low because I couldn't look her in the eye. When I finished, nothing happened. I looked up.

She was dunking a gingernut. I watched her hand rocking back and forth, getting the saturation just right. At the crucial moment, she flipped the biscuit to her mouth, sucking off the soaked part, her tongue worming out for a dribble of tea. It missed. The dribble ran down to her chin and she coughed, giggling. And I had forgotten what I had to say. I knew if I opened my mouth something terrible would dribble out like the tea, gush down the front of my shirt, over her shoes and cover the carpet like
like
like

She sucked her teeth and leaned closer, whispering.

She knew how I felt. Did I think doctor hadn't given her case notes? She knew all about my problems. Did I want her to tell me a true story? Her niece had an accident on her bike once. And she thought, what'll happen if Angela dies? what'll happen? But she prayed to God and the family rallied round and they saw her through to the other side. That's what I had to remember. She knew how I felt; she knew exactly how I felt.

She keeps coming anyway. I make tea and fetch biscuits and we forget all about that first little hiccup. This time she eats only the coffee biscuits so I make a mental note. No more fig rolls. The way I'm coiled is getting uncomfortable. One foot has gone to sleep and my tea is coated. I put it down on the rug and straighten up.

HEALTH VISITOR [Alert to the change] Nothing else to tell me, then?
PATIENT No. Nothing special.

She looks blank and vaguely disappointed. I am not trying.

PATIENT I have a friend visiting tonight. That's all.
HEALTH VISITOR Anyone special? Going out?
PATIENT Just the pub, have a few drinks, that kind of thing.
HEALTH VISITOR Lucky girl. I can't remember the last time someone took me out. Lucky.

She smiles and stands up but guilt is spoiling the relief. I get more guilty as she waddles towards the door, tumbling crumbs from the folds of blue coat, fastening up one top button, ready for outside. My temples thunder as she touches the door and something buzzes in my ear.

You Always Expect Too Much.

The exhaust rattles till she curves out of sight, struggling

23

against her bulk and the need to turn the wheel.

I rub out the creases on the chairs where we have been sitting then take the crockery through and crash it into the sink. One of the red cups has a hairline crack along the rim, fine but deep enough to cut if it wanted. I throw the cup in the bin in case the person it cuts is not me. I lift the biscuits still on the plate and crush them between my hands into the bin. The opened packets follow. They only go soft. The wrappers crackle with life in the recesses of the liner so I let the lid drop fast and turn on the taps to drown it out. They run too hard and soak the front of my shirt. There isn't time to change. I get my coat and run like hell for the stop.

ooo

TESCOs. Red neon all the way to the other end of the precinct, pointing the way to lights, rows of pretty boxes, pastels and primaries, tinsel colours; tins, sealed packets, silver polythene skins begging to be burst. I get dry and warm just thinking about the supermarket. It makes me feel rich and I don't need to think. I can spend hours among the buckle-wheeled trolleys, fruit and fresh vegetables, tins of blueberry pie filling, papaya and mango, numbing my fingers on bags of frozen broccoli and solid chocolate gateaux. The bakery, near the scent and the warmth of the fresh rolls and sugared pastries. The adrenalin smell of coffee drifts and draws towards the delicatessen, the wedges of Edam, Stilton and Danish Blue. But never too long in one place. I don't encourage buying. Sometimes, I get baking things: sugar and flour, dried fruit and tubs of fat, maybe cherries, ginger and peel. Mixed spice, cinnamon, eggs. Or I go to the drinks aisle and read the labels over and over, teasing myself with which one I'll buy. It's always the same one in the end.

Afternoon is easiest. Rush time makes me confused and

anxious. In the afternoon, I feel I belong. There may be a new magazine: full of adverts and recipes, clothes and thin women. A new horoscope. I get excited when I see a new cover smiling over the chewing gum and chocolate at the checkout racks. I buy the magazine and fold it carefully inside my shoulderbag, then walk the length of the precinct, echoing with the ring of my heels, avoiding the skateboards. The end of the mall needs careful handling because people finishing work don't look where they're going. Like clockwork toys. There are days when this makes me furious (I can't get over the inefficiency): other times it makes me depressed. As though I'm trapped in a coop full of hens for the slaughterhouse. Today, the important thing is not to think about the Health Visitor and just keep moving. I lied. No-one is visiting tonight. Or tomorrow night. They did once but not now. I told a lie. I tell lies all the time.

At the end of the precinct, a security guard opens the doors with a leather glove and offers me a sweetie. I smile and take it. Round the corner I drop it in a plastic bin shaped like a rabbit.

Bobby the Bunny says Keep your Country Tidy.

ooo

The first night I spent here alone I thought I heard the doors rattling, something skidding in the mud outside. I went to the police the day after. They told me to sit and someone came beside me with a notebook, speaking slowly. Either they thought I was nervous or a half-wit. Maybe both. But it was a good feeling: it made me warm and docile. I looked at his ring finger and it was naked, spiked with little ginger hairs. He had dark ginger hair cut short at the neck and blond growth like glitter along the jaw. I was trying not to touch him, sitting so close in the dark blue uniform, neat cuffs and collar, holding a pencil and writing down when I spoke. As if I mattered. Then he looked right at me and said,

Do you live alone?
I had to think for a moment.
Yes, I said. Yes. I live alone.
Lot of single women where you are. We'll keep an eye.
Get in touch the minute you suspect anything, any time at
all, day or night. Always sombody here to take a call.
I wondered if he would be kind if he knew me as well as
Mr Dick.
Who do I ask for? I said and he said Graham. Just ask for
Graham.
I wrote it down when I got back. But I never called.

Trees froth in the kitchen window. I fill the water jug at the
tap and don't look outside. I don't put on the stereo this late:
the walls are thin. You can hear the little girl next door
screaming sometimes, close enough to touch. A man and a
woman shouting, effing and blinding and the little girl starts
screaming. It only happens at night. During the day you'd
think the house was deserted. Nobody knows anybody
round here. We keep ourselves to ourselves for our various
reasons.

This is the Way Things Are.

I take the tea through to the livingroom and settle into the
chair. Tonight I know what to do. I have a new magazine.

Jupiter in your sign makes you resilient, but even so,
friends and companions can put a strain on personal cha-
risma at this time. Watch out for new opportunities and
chase any feeling of restriction - you'll regret it later if you
don't. Just remember when the going gets tough, the
tough get going! Big changes are on their way, if you are
patient enough to let them develop.

Baked Alaska - new style.
Making the most of Summer's late harvest.
Our Best Ever Chocolate Cake.
7 Meals that make in Minutes.

26

Diet for a firmer new you!

Converting a Victorian schoolhouse into a des res!

How do the royals keep looking good?

Kiss me Quick Lips - we show you how!

The Last Days of Melyssa: one mother's moving story of heartbreak and a little girl's courage against a crippling disease.

Dear Kathy,
Please help me. My son is an alcoholic. For years, I have tried to block out what I really knew in my heart and so I have to take part of the blame. I never thought he would ever hurt anyone but himself but recently my daughter-in-law has been hinting that he is becoming increasingly violent towards her and the

Dear Kathy,
I have a marvellous husband and two lovely children. My marriage is what I would describe as happy and I have few financial or health worries. But recently, I have begun to watch my family and think about the possibility of some-thing dreadful happening to us. Sometimes the fear has a name, like death or nuclear war; other times, it's nameless. Just something waiting to

Dear Kathy,
My husband and I split up about two years ago. I have rebuilt my life fairly successfully in most respects but one. I miss

Blisters. Little moon craters on the smooth paper. I push the magazine aside and let the tears drip onto the rug until I'm ready to move to the kitchen for some paper towels. My nose fills and drips too, my face will be bloated. I splash my face at the taps and put the kettle on. When I was little, my mother had a big Chinese pattern caddy of tea with a little scoop inside. The scoop said Tea Revives You. I never knew what it meant.

My teeth are chattering. I hold my hands over the kettle spout, feeling the warmth from the burner underneath till the tips of my hair catch. There's a blanket upstairs. I might put on the tv and sit for a while.

Friday Night 7.13.

I say this over a few times but it doesn't make any better sense. The phone rings when I try to write it down and I drop the pencil. I wonder if the phone has anything to do with me writing things down. I listen to it ringing in the empty house. I don't want to answer it but whoever it is might know that's what I'm doing. They might know perfectly well I'm here and not answering deliberately. The phone goes on ringing while I wonder, watching strings of cobweb underneath the stairwell. I'm not cleaning up too well. It goes on ringing. I slip out of my shoes and walk towards it, soundlessly, on my toes. Something dark moves between the railings outside and I wonder if they've been looking in, watching me not answering my own phone. For show, I pick up the receiver. I don't let it touch my mouth. The shouting starts before I say a word.

> IS VIOLET IN? TELL VIOLET I WANT TO SPEAK TO HER. HELLO? IS THAT VIOLET?
> I say I think you have a wrong number.
> NO I DIALLED IT RIGHT. IS THAT NOT VIOLET?
> I say I think you have a wrong number. There is a pause.
> WHO IS THIS SPEAKING? IT'S JIM. IS THAT YOU VIOLET?
> I say Violet's not here. I don't know anyone called Violet. There's no-one of that name here.

28

Then there is only a dull purr on the line. I listen to the purring till it clicks and a howl takes its place, one hollow note.
It could have been Ellen. Or David. Marianne calling all the way from America. But I don't replace the receiver just in case.

Something catches my eye.

A red beachball.
Children on the rim of tile.

Shivering.

A breeze catches my back and I reach for the shirt.
I will burn standing here, breasts heavy in the sun.
My watch makes a gold halo on the towel. Twenty
minutes. I slip the striped cotton over shoulders then
turn back, scanning the trees, the tile. A thin woman
points, her arm an arrow. I follow the line of her
arm.

A group of men stand in a rough O, staring with their
eyes down. Water drips from their arms.

Nothing in the distance. My neck creaks as it turns.

The men float back into the gunsight. Still there,
staring. Something lies among them, flat on the tiles.
My shirt moves and I tilt, dragging towards the
weight. A little boy, five or six, stands with a piece
of the shirt in one brown fist. Tugging.

Signora, signora.

I understand only this word.
He points at the group of men. Their circle grows.

Signora. Your husband is dead.

I look back at the child.
His eyes bloom.

ooo

Saturday.

I dress with great care in front of the mirror.

On Saturday I work with men.

Sometimes Tony collects me, sometimes I walk. Today I somet
walk. The fresh air will do me good.

Mr Poppy says hello. Allan says hello and waves from his
seat behind the grille. Tony raises his eyes and winks. I smile:
it's part of the job. Men cut swathes into the smoke fug to
let me through, some nod. The rest have their backs to me,
scribbling, sucking pens, scanning the papers. I reach the
door at the side of the partition and push it twice because it
always sticks, then go in with the two men behind the bars.
They were expecting me: the heater is burning already. The
chair swivels as you pull it out from under the ledge and you
slot into place. 11.30. I stay in this chair behind the grille for
5 hours. By law a bookie's must not look too inviting.

They're well into their stride by the time I show. Allan sorts and prints numbers into a calculator while Tony puts the slips into piles. Tony counts out the big wins. I am not allowed to give out the big wins because I am only the girl at the till. I ring up the slips and check in winners. Sometimes I write the slips too but most of the men like to write their own. One man writes in gothic script:

St Elmo's Joy : Chepstow

like a medieval bible. Another writes heavy and black, full of backward letters and different sizes. They are regulars. The man who writes beautifully always smiles: the other one doesn't. Sometimes I think they must know I teach.

Allan is buoyant today. He starts telling me jokes between calculations, keeping his voice low because Tony is irritable.

> There are three old men in this geriatric ward
> This whore goes to the priest and says
> This man hasn't had sex for ages and he

His face lights up when he tells these jokes. Any other way, he looks wrong. At the funeral, sweltering in a black suit and tie he settled down on the grass and offered me a job in the bookie's. Pleasure in breaking little rules. He tells the jokes loudly because of Tony's mood. Tony knows. He moves between us, disturbing the punchlines deliberately.
      A lot on the 2.30. How's the till?
He checks his value for money every so often by keeping us at work.

The phone rings and he steps aside to answer while Allan makes a face behind his back. Code-named punters place bets long-distance: Tony takes the calls, rings up their slips himself, making me wait with mine. He tries to do every-one's job when he's edgy. I move back from the till to let him take over and make coffee for the men. Mr Poppy stops chalking up prices and comes over when he hears the kettle: he always says Thank You. Tony doesn't drink coffee. He

31

goes through the afternoon on sugar doughnuts and cherry cola so his smiles are small and sticky. When I dole out the cups, I notice they are all wearing the same golfing jumpers and neat slacks. Tony takes this as a compliment, then squeezes close to my chair when I sit down again. There's not much room behind the grille.

By 2.00 the slips arrive at once, pushing through the bars with hands attached, waiting for change while I ring up, putting the stamped slips in a heap for Tony. He fills racks behind me.

I remind people to take their change. Sometimes I ring up the wrong thing and the men have to be patient with me. They nod in a longsuffering way among themselves. They prefer to deal with the men. They gather at the mesh and chat with Allan and Tony, the businessmen. If they see me looking, they get shy, smile and joke to cover up. They are reassured by my ringing up wrong numbers. Tony strokes my hair when he's in a good mood and tells them I'm a pet.

By four o'clock, there's just me and Tony. He leans over while I'm filing slips.

Doing anything special tonight?
Just the usual, I say.
I never know whether this is a real question or not.
Taking the dog up to the track in Glasgow, he says. Big race. Gets the blood going.

I smile because I'm not sure what to say. He has a greyhound: Allan says he gives it more attention than he gives his wife. I've never heard his wife's name. The dog's called Tony's Queen.
Ever been to the track?
He levels his eyes on me and I drop mine. I shake my head, beginning to feel uncomfortable. I feel him looking at me through the top of my head.
I'll take you one day, he says. I think you'd be surprised. Owner's enclosure, champagne if she wins. Touch of style.

He's wearing a quart of aftershave. I told him once his

aftershave smelled nice for something to say and he wears more and more of it every week. I turn and put more slips in the boxes.

Great, I say. I'm not sure if he's serious or not but make sure I answer as though it's an obvious joke. He pats my head again, holds out my money. He keeps holding it when I try to take it from him and says, Say please to Tony.

I raise my eyes but blush and spoil the effect. I'm supposed to smile and I do. He laughs and lets it go. I don't get to put on my coat without his helping hand. Someone comes into the shop, a late customer. I shout cheerio and walk fast. I walk past the bus stop and keep going. Out of sight of the bookie's I run.

Bars clash into place as I look into the windows. Clothes suspended as though the limbs have withered away, lights dimming behind. Sheets go over the dummies. Tea-time. Panic drives me to the top of the hill, wheezing like an old horse to wait outside Ellen's door, my hand in mid-air, catching my breath before I knock. Mist gathers back where the town was, frosting the light round the streetlamps. Blue smoke belches from the cars at the foot of the hill and the clatter of high heels on the pavements seems louder than usual, even at this distance. I steel myself and knock.

Light spills into the porch as Ellen arrives, her white hair ragged. She was probably sleeping at the fire. I say I hope I haven't woken her up and she says not at all, not at all. The hall smells of simmered soup, new baking. I tell her it's a short visit. Regardless, she brings wedges of sticky lemon sponge with the coffee, several sticks of shortbread: I know they have been made for me. I take a piece and make a show of appreciation: I can't refuse. Ellen makes things because it is how she cares. She clucks and tells me I'm getting thin. She watches me smile at the cake, not knowing what it's costing, and sips her coffee, spreading her knees for the heat.

So how was work? she asks.

Not so busy, I say. I prefer it busy so I don't get bored.

Your eyes look bloodshot. She peers at me. All that smoke.

I know.

I don't say they've been like that for the past two days. Defensive, I take my first bite into the cake. The sugar crunches and spills onto my jeans, crumbs flake away. I force away the fear over and over as I keep chewing. I finish the whole piece before I notice, and suck the sugar from my fingers. It tastes the way cake does when you're seven. Wonderful. I want more but know I won't take any. There will be a price to pay for this as it is.

Anything interesting happen today?

She's expansive now, leaning back into her chair with the knitting because I've eaten the cake. It makes her feel good.

Tony said he might take me to see a dog track.

That should be interesting, she says, meaning the opposite. What's he like?

She means is he married and should I be letting strange men talk about race-tracks to me. I pretend I misunderstand the question and tell her he has a moustache. Mentioning it was a mistake.

She smiles from the chair, shortbread crumbs on the corners of her mouth. The knitting light angled to her face makes her skin translucent, her cheeks pink. She lifts her knitting and begins dipping and folding strands of hairy yellow wool. It'll make Marianne look like a car sponge. Ellen sees me looking and holds it up to the light.

Just something for Marianne's Christmas. Think she'll like it? Such a pretty colour.

Ellen.

Sometimes I forget and call her Mrs Holmes. She came home from an outing to Skye and found me in her house, sedated to hell in the kitchen, Marianne trying to explain why. Ellen's whole face melted. I remember watching

34

her face changing and having to acknowledge then that something was wrong. I was still having to remind myself every five minutes what it was. Seven weeks later we took Marianne to the station together because Ellen doesn't drive. London was too far away so we saw her off on a Glasgow train. We stood on the platform watching as Marianne got smaller, waving. It felt put-on, something out of a bad TV film. I couldn't believe she was going far: you never go too far on an island. Eventually you reach water.

Afterwards we went to a cafe near the station. It was dirty and the coffee was bad. There was a juke-box and I wanted to put on something loud and raucous. Spite. But Ellen isn't the rock-music type. She's not even the cafe type. Neither of us was particularly chatty. I knew Marianne would have said something about keeping an eye on me, but I didn't ask. I didn't want Ellen to feel awkward, to have to admit she'd been conscripted. So I said something about hoping Marianne was going to like it there, America.

Ellen said, She would have stayed if she could. She wanted to stay. But the arrangements had all been made. No-one could have guessed.
We agreed on that one. I told her nobody needed to worry about me. I said it was better she was going, sticking to her plans. Besides, staying wouldn't change anything.

But she didn't want to leave, really. Not when you're like this.
That surprised me. I wasn't like anything then. You couldn't tell there was anything wrong with me at all. But we played to each other what we thought sounded best: as though we were being overheard.

Ellen's eyes loom over the tops of her specs.
Have you another appointment with Dr Stead this week?
I look up from the fire. Her eyes are on the stitches. Lattice patterns of yellow fabric.
Monday. After school.
How does he think you are these days?
Doesn't say much. I have to get more of the red pills,

35

though I still have plenty of the other ones. He's still sending that woman to the house.

That's not so bad, then.

We wait a minute, listening to the fire.

Is she doing you any good?

She's very nice, I say, my eyes on the needles, the yellow lace falling from her hands.

I walk back before she eats her meal and I feel I have to stay. The evening is already darkening, getting chill. I cross the stretch of moorland, the bridges over the motorway, the wasteland development. The workmen are clearing up for the night and shout across. I pretend I don't hear and keep walking. I let my hand rest on my thigh as I walk, feeling the muscle tighten and firm. Walking is always terrible.

ooo

Closing the door is a calm affair but I am dizzy, hair spiky with the cold and the wind outside, reeking of smoke. The shops are closed and don't open tomorrow. A picture appears in my head: cement and brick. I am walled in like an adulterous nun till Monday. The garden from the kitchen window looks like a set for a film about Passchendale. I make tea. The thought of the cake in my stomach makes me sweat.

What will I do while I'm lasting, Marianne? What will I do?

The day Marianne left, I found a note pinned to the kitchen wall. It was there when I came back from the airport without her along with some books of poems, addresses, a foreign phone number, money and a bottle of gin. The gin and the money went long since. The note is still there.

THINGS YOU CAN DO IN THE EVENING.
listen to the radio
watch TV
have a bath
listen to records
read
write letters or visit
go for a walk
sew
go out for a meal
phone someone nice

I hear every radio programme at least twice. I can recite the news by the time I go to bed. Besides I have to move around while I'm listening. This is not an occupation on its own.

TV is tricky: the news is depressing and the programmes sometimes worse. I hate adverts. They are full of thin women doing exercises and smiling all the time. They make me guilty.

The water takes ages for a bath. I hate waiting.

It's asking for trouble to listen to music alone.

I already read everything. I read poems and plays and novels and newspapers and comic books and magazines. I read tins in supermarkets and leaflets that come through the door, unsolicited mail. None of it lasts long and it doesn't give me answers. Reading too fast is not soothing.

Writing is problematic. I cover paper with words as fast as painting. Sometimes it's indecipherable and I throw it away.

Visiting is awkward. The place I live is an annexe of nowhere and besides, I don't like to wish myself on anyone.

Walking is awful. I do that when I want to feel worse. I always run.

Sewing and going for a meal. Tricky juxtaposition.

I used to sew a lot. It occupied me. During the day I went to school and in the evenings I cut cloth. I cut cloth into shapes from paper and then sewed it together again. Needles punctured pincushions into my finger ends and left little scratches on my wrists alongside the bruises from shifting furniture, sears from the oven and tears in my nails from cleaning. Domestic wounds. I sewed at the table from when I came back from work to when I thought bed-time should be. At intervals, according to the clock, I would prepare something to eat: maybe a can of soup, a sandwich. Functional food. One evening, I was so intent on a hem, I forgot. When I did look at my watch, it was well after the usual meal-time. Hunger hadn't interrupted. I sat and thought about this for a while.

There was a can of vegetable soup in the cupboard: individual size. I found the opener and dug it into the top, lifting it higher with each turn of the handle. Some of the stuff inside smeared on my knuckle. It felt slimy, unpleasant. Inside the can the surface was a kind of flattened jelly, dark red with bits of green and yellow poking through. Watery stuff like plasma started seeping up the sides of the viscous block. It didn't look like food at all. I slid one finger into it to the depth of a nail. The top creased and some of the pink fluid slopped up and over the jagged lip of the can. It was sickening but pleasantly so. Like a little kid playing with mud. The next thing I knew, I'd pushed my hand right inside the can. The semi-solid mush seethed and slumped over the sides and onto the worktop as my nails tipped the bottom and the torn rim scored the skin. I had to withdraw carefully. Soup stung into the cuts so I used my other hand and scooped up as much of the mess as I could and cradled it across the room, red soup and blood dripping onto the lino. There, my cupped hands over the sink, I split my fingers and let the puree slither, spattering unevenly onto the white porcelain. I was learning something as I stared at what I was doing; the most obvious thing yet it had never dawned on me till I stood here, bug-eyed at the sink, congealing soup up to my wrists. I didn't need to eat.
I didn't need to eat.

The first four days were the worst. After that, it found its own level. I occasionally still cut cloth in the evenings, now without interruption. Not tonight. I'm too tired to force myself to stay in one place. Only the phone is left. I can't face the phone tonight either.

Perfect Pasta in minutes
No-nonsense looks for the Working Mum
The Lie that Tells the Truth

Nothing better get in your way this month, cos you mean business! Something that's been irritating you for a while finally gets its chance to see the light of day. Meanwhile, those around you are in for a rough ride: be careful or you'll say something you might regret later. Especially if it's to someone close. Your love life is on an upturn - maybe all that drive is packing you with

Last month's. No good.
But then it's all no good. It's all no fucking good.

A scared little boy hisses through salt-white teeth.

The backs of the men grow nearer as I walk. My feet lift from the ground making no sound. I am un-no-ticeable. The poolside crowds with people who don't see me. I say nothing, shouldering between oblivious people, smiling all the time. And there is someone lying on the tile.
White marble against the red slats.

The low hum of voices makes the smile wider. I am not in control of my face. The tongue moves inside the soft skull.

39

It's all right now
It's all right

and something starts
                    starts

*I look down and his mouth is a red O. White water
runs through his hair.*

His mouth is a red O, eyes wide to the sky.

ooo

I watch the ceiling till it's light enough to make lists.
Sunday Mornings I make a lot of lists.

I stay in bed because it's warmer and pile the cover with
books, magazines and bits of writing paper, drinking tea till
I'm sloshing like a water bomb. Then it's time to get up for
the Sunday papers - I can spend a while cutting out things
to put in the post. I listen to The Archers, Pick of the Week,
Desert Island Discs. I make more tea and eject the week's
newspapers, the debris of last night's clippings then carry
the junk to the kitchen.

On Sundays, I bake.

The kitchen scales are good ones, a present from Ellen.
Fractions of ounces and grammes if I need them: I like to be
meticulous when I bake. I make good gingerbread, wonderful sponge. My shortbread melts in the mouth because I take
care. I think of mouths when I'm baking, digging my fingers

into the flour and fat, blending eggs and sugar and milk. Greasing tins makes my hands reek and clogs my nails with melting margarine.

The glass jars are polished every day, so the kitchen glitters. Muscatel, Lexia, pitted dates, candied peel, cherries and chocolate chips; quicksands of brown sugars. The powders make clouds: wholemeal, wheatmeal, strong plain white and brown, granary, rye and buckwheat for blinis. I'm very adventurous. I fold and whisk and knead for hours among the jars, dropping blended mixes from spoons into the shining tins. I read the ingredients and the method out loud for the beautiful sound of the words. In two hours there will be a Dundee cake, Ginger squares, Oatmeal scones and Fresh Orange Tarts. After that I might make preserves. A good wife going to waste.

I lived with a man for the better part of seven years. We met at school: fifth form romance. Our first date was in a cafe when we should have been in French. We ate salad rolls and doughnuts that tasted like sacred wafer because we were out of school and we both liked the same things: doughnuts and salad rolls. Once we went late into school eating opposite ends of an eclair, giggling, faces too close, smeared with chocolate icing and cream. Half way across the playground, a stray teacher caught sight of us. He shouted SEPARATE YOURSELVES and sliced the air between us with the flat of his hand. We separated. He said we were a terrible example.

I wiped the cream off my nose as defiantly as I could and said I couldn't see why. He stopped short.

Pardon? he said.

Look, I said. You're holding a cigarette. That's a worse example to impressionable young minds than anything we're doing.

I knew it wouldn't make things any better but I couldn't stop. Paul kept his mouth shut and looked apologetic. We got hell. Paul never ate eclairs in the playground with me again. He always did have a better instinct for keeping out of trouble.

We had bad times and we had good times on and off over the seven years. I learned to cook good meals and run a house. The fridge was always well stocked and the cupboards interesting. I cleaned the floors and the rings round the bath that showed where we had been but I knew there was something missing. I felt we were growing apart. We were. It was called growing up but I didn't know that at the time. I tried to talk to him because the magazines I was reading said communication was important. He was reading different magazines: his magazines told him different things altogether. I thought the answer was soul-searching and he thought it was split-crotch knickers. Stalemate. We were unhappy. He punished me for his unhappiness by refusing to touch me. Night after night. I punished him for my unhappiness by not speaking but I hadn't the same willpower. His willpower lasted out for months. A year. More. Practice was making him perfect and me desperate for kisses. I had an affair. I couldn't see it wasn't the sex I missed so much as someone to care whether I missed it or not. The affair didn't help. Paul found out because he read my letters when I wasn't in and knew everything I was doing. I didn't know he was doing that and thought he had xray vision. I thought I was going crazy. I started writing my diary in code. I started thinking in code because I thought he could tap my brain. I became afraid to leave the flat in case he could tell things by feeling the walls when I was out or maybe through supervision. I thought he was Superman. I couldn't live with Superman without thinking

    a) Superman's weaknesses are my fault (like Kryptonite) and

    b) I was vastly inferior in every respect.

He talked to me even less and I talked to myself more and more. He still ate my meals and let me make the beds, do his washing and attend to the Superflat but it wasn't the same. Now there was no talk at all, only the sound of two people suffocating into different pillows. We were killing each other. There was nobody to ask for help because I was too proud and too ashamed I wasn't fit to live with. My mother was dying and it wasn't right to speak to her about this kind of thing. That was a romantic idea. Even if she had been well, I wouldn't have said anyway. Besides, I needed his car to supervise my mother's dying. They always build hospitals a million miles away from people.

The day of the funeral, he shook my hand in line with everybody else waiting outside the crematorium. I looked at his face and couldn't think who he was for a minute. It didn't feel better when I remembered. It felt worse. But still I stayed in his flat, where there was nothing of mine, nothing of me. I got more and more guilty about sapping his Superpowers and thought I couldn't cope. I knew I had to leave and I had to get help. I found a shoulder to cry on. The shoulder thought I might be more comfortable crying in bed. Paul found out about this too. He wanted to hurt me so he told me he was screwing everything in skirts within a fifteen-mile radius. I told him it was a source of comfort to know I hadn't inflicted permanent damage on his erectile tissue. That was when he played his ace.

I don't need you for anything, he said, loud and flat. I don't need you for a thing.
I racked my brain to find something to prove it wasn't true. I came up with the only answer left.
Look, I'm going to make us something to eat. At least I can do that much. You need me all right. You need me because you can't cook. You can't fucking cook.
I yelled too.

He went out slamming the door but I made something anyway. Pasta with seafood sauce, garlic bread, olive and pepper salad: his favourites. I didn't have favourites: I liked what he liked. I thought he had great taste. He'd come back sooner or later.
He came back an hour later with a carrier bag. A Chinese take-away. For one. He ate it without looking at me but I heard the message loud and clear.

SHOVE YOUR FOOD

It took me a month to find somewhere else to live. He was right. He didn't need me for a thing.

I don't think I ever came to terms with the shock. Even while

43

I decorated my new home, I took time out to make him a cake now and again, some homemade preserves. These days he stays away. He has someone else who cooks his meals. The cupboard under the sink bulges with chutney.

The cakes come, transformed from the oven. The scent of them cooling on the wire rack makes me feel weak. When they stop steaming I can wrap them in silver foil because they are gifts, and put them away in the cupboard. They make me feel secure in there: ready for other people to eat and me to ignore. A strength. That gives me a lift.

I make a note about the appointment with Dr Stead tomorrow because I'm confident after the baking. I can handle thinking about him right now, so I make my list of things to say tomorrow so I don't forget anything while I'm there.

DO I HAVE TO TAKE THE RED THINGS?
(I read in a magazine anti-depressants make you fat. I've been terrified of them ever since.)
PLEASE STOP SENDING HV
ARE THE SLEEPING PILLS SUPPOSED TO WORK?
STILL NO BLEEDING.

It looks assertive because of the capitals. I'll need it tomorrow. I need all the help I can get with Dr Stead.

ooo

I put the heating on and my skin starts rippling. The house is clean from Friday but I polish a little extra to be sure. Then I go to the shop at the end of the road and buy cheese, bread, milk: things to make the fridge look populated. By five the water is ready. I go upstairs. It's time for the bathing ritual. Preparation for the nightvisitor.

> Dear Kathy,
> I know you're going to think this is a silly worry
> but it's not to me. I have a very understanding
> boyfriend and we both want to make love, but
> every time the occasion arises, I'm not able to "let
> go". I can't tell him what it is because I'm too
> ashamed. But I'm scared he'll be repulsed when
> he sees me or that I'll do something stupid. Even
> when we're kissing I worry about being a mess
> afterwards, not what he thought I was under the
> make-up. Please help me. This is ruining my
> chance of happiness.

All sorts of people came at first. I wasn't even in the right
place but they found me. People can be very kind. It screws
me up. Marianne did the talking and they paid calls. Some
of the people I thought would come didn't but others came
to take their place. There were compensations.

Sam came.
He had a new bike and a new face: scrappy bits of beard and
broken veins on his cheeks. He took me out to see the new
bike: silver and red, shiny chrome, smell of hot grease. I
wore Michael's leather jacket and we went out, way out
along the coast to some pub or other. Mhairi and Sean were
there, Frank and Joyce. Me with my hair plastered down
and my eyes streaming from the wind. Sam bought me gin.
Sean bought me gin. Frank, Joyce and Mhairi bought me
gin. We sat round a space-invader table and looked at the
shapes moving, luminous green and yellow through the
glass top. Sam took me back on the motorway to open her
up and wind rushing towards us took my breath away: I
yelled all the way to the estate.

It was a surprising time. I spent nights rambling in strange
cars, eating meals with people I hardly knew. But I was
relieved when it tailed off. It made me worry too much and

45

I was never as grateful as I wanted to be. It made me tense and anxious wondering why they came, why they did it. I got guilty about wondering. I kept thinking there is no such thing as a free lunch and wondering when the price came. It didn't but I was easier when it stopped anyway.

There is No Such Thing as a Free Lunch.
There is no such thing as Lunch.
Joke.

Now I have particular visits. I don't like to take anything for granted. This Sunday night he's coming round. Maybe I will be embraced, entered, made to exist. The physical self is precarious.

The Bathing Ritual.
The bathwater must be hot: warm isn't good enough. I wait till the water is scalding and run the bath as evening falls, getting rid of the day's clothes: standing in the steam, acclimatising.
I pour oil into the scalding water. My skin gets creaky and dry as I get thinner, like tracing paper: the oil will make me smooth. I step into the water, careful because of the heat. The mirror cuts off my head as I sit and steady my lungs, feeling the flesh under the surface turn raw. When sweat breaks on my upper lip, I can't see the mirror for steam. The scent of the oil is lost among the clouds.
On the white bath rim, the wash glove
                            the soap.
The glove is made of matting, knotted in rows. I dip it once into the water and pass it over the soap: only once so the hair doesn't coat, flatten out against the cloth.

When I finish, the skin sizzles: my whole surface sings. I stand up in the bath draining away the ordinariness that floats with the scum on the water, rinse myself with fresh water from the taps. The cold water runs on while I sit and soap each leg in turn, then lift the razor, checking the edge is keen. It gives a better finish slicing upward, against the hair: it severs more closely. I have to be careful it doesn't catch or draw blood. That would be unsightly. The water runs down each foreleg while I shave, carrying the shed animal hair away down the black hole under the taps. Fleeced, I turn off the taps and step out to rub my skin hard with the flat loops of the towel till it hurts. This makes me warmer. Then I stoop to wash my hair over the basin, pouring lukewarm cupfuls till the water is clear again. Twice. I wrap the damp hair in a towel and wipe a place in the misted mirror.

Boxes and bottles on the bedroom floor: creams, fluids, cotton and paper. Moisturiser. To keep in the juice. Glutinous stuff for my elbows, knees and knuckles in case they're rough. I pluck my eyebrows, the single hair on my upper lip. Nail-scissors to make my pubic hair neat. Perfume for my ears, my neck, my wrists and navel; the flat space between my breasts, tips of my spine, between the toes. I file my nails, hands and feet with emery and pumice, pushing back the cuticles, defining whiteness with chalk. I paint my toenails. The radio mutters a play under the fallen bedspread. I paint them again. Then each fingernail the same way. I leave my armpits free from chemical interference: deodorant matts, it tastes bad. This is my token to naturalness in case this is what he prefers. I stand and pad on some talc from a canister instead, dripping white dust onto my knees and belly, puffs of smoke across my chest. I put on my prettiest underwear: net lace and satin, ribbon straps. Black. I wear a lot of black.

I pick up the hairdryer.

Not long now. I sit on the bedspread and spread out the things for my face. This has to be subtle; just enough makeup to make my eyes seem more, the lips rounder, bleach out the circles and lines growing like a web under the lashes. I have to tint my face because I am pale in cold weather, powder blue. This is unappetising and nothing to kiss. I tint myself Peaches and Dream, stain my eyelids lilac, brush the lashes black. I smear my lips with clear wax from a stick (red is too vivid and leaves marks, so may make him cautious). I am to be entirely inviting in case. In case. I check the watch again. I never know what to wear. I'm still combing and fixing earrings by the time I hear the grind of wheels outside, the low purr of the engine.

Sunday Night 9.05.
It's important not to think about Monday.

Bright light flashes past the window and the engine cuts. I think about his hands on the wheel, red hair at the rim of his cuff. He is always late, but he comes. The engine stops as I test a smile in the mirror; it is difficult to pull the thing together, to see all of the offering and not a jumble of separate parts. I don't think I want to anyway. Footfalls thud on the boards downstairs. I smile at the woman in the mirror. Her eyes are huge. But what looks back is never what I want. Someone melting. And too much like me.

She switches out the light and opens the door.

> *In the white corridor*
> *over and over, the same thing*
> *something thudding*
> *thudding solid behind the door*
>
> > *say there's nothing*
> > *say there's nothing say there's*
> > *jesus*
> > *jesus*
> > *jesus*

a tall dark boy comes towards me
heavy accent and these still brown eyes
and there's a terrible sound of

my mouth is open

> *jesus*
> *say there's nothing*
> *say there's nothing*
> *say there's*

> > *terrible sound of*
> > *thudding in my chest and someone*

> > *screaming*
> > *screaming*
> > *scream*

ooo

Mondays.
The smoke out of my hair, the creases of leftover makeup
under my eyes, aftershave and stale perfume. Pile-up on the
M6, beached whales in Alaska, earthquake in Chile. Screams
and falling in the dark.

sometime

Blaze through work by all means but be circumspect. You'd
be surprised how much cumuppance tends to follow even
little mistakes. Scottish Education: apportion blame that ye
have not blame apportioned unto you. It wisny me, it was
you/ him/ her/ a wee man and he ran away. No relief when
the bell rings. My lift with the women tells me *Dennis*

wouldn't eat the liver after all what did I tell you not even with the onions and Evelyn Little's wedding eh must be at least thirty six by this etc etc. They never open the windows and me in a poloneck to hide the weals, the way adolescents do. The car goes too near to the verge when she says *he never speaks he's out on that garage or the golf course the whole time and never speaks at all.*

Leaves scratch at the window.
You raise your hand to touch them before you remember.

ooo

Seven minutes early.
The appointments line snakes right out the door and into the drizzle. I go to Dr Stead too often and feel bad about it. I always think I'm wasting his time and I hate that so sometimes the visits are acrimonious. So I always go early and make notes. It's supposed to make me businesslike and brisk. It's supposed to save his time and my anxiety about it, but it never works out like that. It works out like this:

DOCTOR How are things/what's new/ how's the week been
treating you?

I try to remember the things in the notepad. They get jumbled and I think I'm going to cry. This is terrible so I say anything.

PATIENT I'm not sleeping. I'm still not sleeping.
DOCTOR Try taking the yellow things an hour earlier in the
evening. And the red things later. There's nothing
left to do to the green things on this theme. Keep
them as they were. [Already writing prescription]
Do you need more?

PATIENT Thank-you. I feel terrible.

DOCTOR Well, let's leave it for a while, see how you are next
week. One thing at a time, eh?

I come out like a steamrollered cartoon: two-dimensions to
start with then flattened some more till I'm tissue. I walk to
the bus stop with my head down. Even on warm days I take
a scarf to hide my face.

Dr Stead's in the upstairs surgery today.
He's never anywhere else but the receptionist always says it
as though it's a temporary arrangement for the doctor to be
in the upstairs surgery. It proves her indispensability as the
only one who knows for sure where he is. You know she's
hoping one day you get too cocky and go upstairs without
her say-so and find someone else there instead. So I always
take the advice as if it's news: I'm not going to be the one
who gets caught out.
Take your cards with you please.

I take them and say nothing. Once, I called her Mrs McKay
by mistake. It says Mrs McKay on her lapel badge so I
thought it would be all right. She looked right through me
as if I wasn't there and shouted NEXT so maybe it wasn't
her name at all, or if it was, she just didn't like people using
it. She likes to keep the patients on their toes. Or maybe it's
her revenge for all the coughing and wheezing and scratching she has to put up with. Anyway, I don't speak now, just
names and dates. I take my cards and go upstairs to wait.

Preparation for the Doctor:
A short exercise lasting anything up to forty minutes.

[The surgery is blue. The patient stands while the doctor
scratches his neck, sits, rifles through pieces of paper. Some
of the pieces of paper fall and he picks them up, sighs, grins
tightly to himself, scratches the back of his neck with his ring
finger then looks up.]

DOCTOR Sit. [Pause] So how are things what's new who are

51

you anyway?

PATIENT I'm tired and I still need somebody to talk to. I need to get less angry about everything. I'm going nuts.

DOCTOR Don't tell me how to do my job. Relax. You can talk to me. I made a double appointment so we can have twenty minutes. Go ahead. I'm listening.

PATIENT What can I say that makes sense in twenty minutes?

DOCTOR Try. You're not trying. You're looking for something that doesn't exist, that's why you're not happy. Look at me. I'm under no illusions. That's why I'm in control.

PATIENT How can I be more like you?

DOCTOR That's not what I meant. that's not what I meant at all. Envy is a destructive emotion. Besides I had to fight hard to get to feel like this. I'm buggered if I'm giving away the fruits of my hard work for nothing. You must tell me how you are.

PATIENT I don't seem to know how I am except bad. There's nothing there but anger and something scary all the time. I don't want to get bitter because it will ruin my looks.

DOCTOR Maybe a hobby would help. Facetiousness is not an attractive trait in a young woman.

PATIENT I know I know. I can't help myself.

DOCTOR OK. We'll try these green ones for a change. And step up the anti-depressants. Don't drink or drive. Make an appointment for a few days time and try to be more helpful in future.

While I try to imagine him shouting the last bit, he comes out the surgery and takes in a little boy with a huge sty on one eye. Maybe he guesses I sit out here rehearsing.

IMPATIENT OK, let's talk straight. You ask me to talk then you look at your watch. What am I supposed to take from that? This whole thing is ridiculous. Can't you send me to someone who's paid to have me waste their time? You don't know what to do with me but you keep telling me to come

52

	back. And stop sending that woman to see me. All it does is make me guilty and secretive.
DOCTOR	Look, this is reactive depression. I don't see that sending you to a specialist will help things. Talk to your family if you can't talk to me.
IMPATIENT	I have no family.
DOCTOR	Don't be melodramatic.

There's a click and a scuffle. Dr Stead is standing in the doorframe of the surgery waiting with his appointment sheet. He looks smaller than he was in my head. Crow's feet are beginning to dent his temples and his nails are bitten into the quick. We try to be at ease and go through the routine about the pills, the anxiety, the sleeplessness, etc. There is no consensus, no conclusion. No answer. When he reaches for the prescription pad, something like warm fingertips slither under my chin. They gather, cool and drip making dark spots on my trousers. This is unavoidable but still humiliating. I leak steadily over his nice chair.

There's another prescription here for when you leave.
He sighs and holds out a kleenex. I'm his last patient and it's probably been a long day.
Are you listening to me?
I nod and he goes on. I don't want to look up. He must see a lot of this sort of thing. Like me, he is familiar with it. He gives up with the kleenex and we each pretend to the other it isn't happening. Professionals.
Good. No word from the referral yet?
I shake my head.
Let's see. Nearly a fortnight. I still don't agree with you about the usefulness of Health Visitors but it's obvious things aren't getting much better. We'll hang on for Foresthouse.

I think about things not getting any better, knowing fine that THINGS = ME. He sighs. I know he's hating this. He knows I know.
You must understand they're always busy, though. They'll take a few days to write. Hospitals always do these days.

53

It's already been a fortnight.

He stands up. I gather up the prescription and follow him to the door. He always opens it for me: one of the old school. Just before he opens it, he reminds me not to expect miracles.

No, I say.

No.

An old man is sitting in the corridor. He pulls his coat tighter and looks across to me, irritated at being seen waiting.

I've been waiting half an hour.

He coughs.

Bloody doctors. Think you've nothing better to be doing. He is not talking to me. He is talking just in case anyone is watching, waiting, to call him to account. Or just for something to say. When the doctor comes the old man will say nothing. The doctor is an educated man. He is doing his best. The old man is merely old.

Bastards, he says.

He has to blame someone. He blames the empty corridor. When the doctor comes he will be like the rest of us and smile. When the doctor says he's sorry to have kept him waiting, he'll say Not at all, doctor, not at all. I keep my head down, expecting something sudden to fall from the sky at any minute. I jerk, ducking the impact that never comes.

ooo

A fortnight before she left, Marianne took me out in the car. We had a huge bottle of cheap wine. I held it cooling out of the window while she drove. Irresponsible. It was very late: hardly any cars. We went for miles into the country past Kilmarnock till she cut the engine and we sat in the dark drinking the wine and looking up at half the moon. She was worried about going and wanted to make me think about lasting through. We drank lots of wine and decided it was all about lasting through, just getting on with the day to day

54

till it got less terrible. I wanted to know what would happen if she hated the States.

I'll come back, she said.

Her shoulders tightened. She was being flippant because she was worried too. She was worried about lasting out at least a year in a strange place with people who would make a big thing out of not understanding her accent. Even if it was the worst job in the world she wouldn't be able to quit: she had signed contracts that said so.

We had some more wine.

At least I'll be paid good money for hating it.

This time it came out bitter. We ran out of things to say so we went home, weaving down the centreline on the road back, over the motorway and down onto the sand of Irvine shore. She stopped the car to look at the sea: there is no sea in Kentucky. Then she turned and looked at me.

Just last out. Last out for me. It has to get better eventually.

I know, I said. I know that.

The sound of the waves carried all the way across the dunes.

But what will I do while I'm lasting, Marianne? What will I do?

I don't want to

> listen to the radio
> watch tv
> have a bath
> listen to records
> read
> write letters or visit
> go for a walk
> sew
> go out for a meal
> for reasons I already explained.

That leaves the phone.

Marianne is one of life's natural phoners. My own feelings are mixed. My mother didn't have one at home: too expensive. I spent my whole teenage life without a phone.

But I thought they must be wonderful. I thought everybody had one but us and owning one was a sure sign of success. Smooth plastic casing, seductive coil of wire and complacent purr when you lifted the receiver: the whole thing was desirable. I didn't really think about what it was for: that wasn't the point.

The point was
The point was
The point

I didn't know the point. Only the desire mattered.

There was a phone in Paul's flat, ready fitted. One of these little Wimpey numbers with just one big room to live in but there was a phone. Already, attachment to a man meant better things. I was upwardly mobile: phone number all my own. More or less. I couldn't call my mother since she still didn't have one but I could call the speaking clock and the operator. I could call work to say when I was ill: this didn't happen often. Not then. I would get excited if it rang and run dripping from the bath to find out who was on the other side. Most times it was Paul saying he was working late. Then I paid for my mother to have a phone: she was ill and I thought it was a good idea. She called me more often than I called her. She called me since it seemed ungrateful not to after I had paid all the money. She always held it too far away from her mouth and shouted. Sometimes it rang in the middle of the night and scared her. She was never sure who it was. Overnight, she left it off the hook. In case.
Soon, I had to phone the hospital to talk to her. More than once she didn't know who I was. This must have been frightening but I kept doing it. I called her once from the top of a mountain, shouting I'M CALLING YOU FROM THE TOP OF A MOUNTAIN as if it was significant. She hung up. She didn't remember when I told her about it a week later. Someone rang me at work the day she died. I went to the house and checked the phone, the one I paid for, on the hall table. It was off the hook.

I got a phone for the cottage the day I moved in. After all, I thought, everyone needs a phone. You can't live nowadays without a phone. Michael would call late in the night after his wife had gone to bed and whisper down the line to my bedroom. Then there was the call that began with only two words.

She knows.

When he put the receiver down I threw up. I just missed the phone.

I phoned Norma straight off the Spanish flight at Heathrow. A noisy callbox, waiting for the Glasgow connection. I wanted her to know what I did. First hand. Rumour and speculation can do awful things.

Marianne phoned people all the time after that to let them know. Norma was doing a lot of the same thing. You could hear the embarrassment in their voices at being told again. She had plenty of time. It took three weeks to get him back in a lead-sealed box. All that time, she was phoning.

The phone is an instrument of intrusion into order. It is a threat to control. Just when you think you are alone and safe, the call could come that changes your life. Or someone else's. It makes the same flat, mechanical noise for everyone and gives no clues what's waiting there on the other end of the line.

You can never be too careful.

ooo

I was alone in the house and the phone rang. The wind howled and the doors knocked with absent hands, tapping with the draught upstairs. Something fell, thudded against the floor in the empty room through the ceiling and trailed itself across the boards up there.

I was alone in the house. And the phone rang.

PHONE   Who's there? [Deep breathing] Who is this?
ME   I live here.
PHONE   Speak to me. Who is this?
ME   I live here. You phoned me. Tell me who you are.
PHONE   Speak to me. Somebody said you were sick.
ME   I think you have a wrong number.
PHONE   Don't give me that. Speak to me, don't you want to speak to me?
ME   [Swallowing: trying to sound firm] Leave me alone.
PHONE   Don't be silly. I'm your sister. Don't you want to talk to your sister. I'm the only sister you've got. I'm your sister for chrissakes.

The smell of heavy scent like sugarwater clogged up my nose and made me want to faint only I never faint. I knew she knew it was me. She knew I knew.

ME   [Helpless] Hello. How are you?
MYRA   Can't complain. I have this dog now. Trixie. She has a mucous infection. Trixie. But the thing is what about you. Somebody said you were sick. I'm worried about you. Somebody told me you were sick.
ME   [Grotesque effort to sound devilmaycare] No. Do I sound sick? No. I'm fine, fine. I'm OK really. Nothing wrong with me. I'm fine. Great. Do I sound sick?
MYRA   You sound funny. Are you still working in that school?
ME   Yep. Still there. I'm fine. You don't need to worry about me.
MYRA   Tell me where you live. I want to come round.
ME   Well, it's hard to do that right now.

If I gave her another address she would know it was false and find me anyway. She could track me down and punch me to death. Myra's like that. She could just stand and scare me to death.

MYRA	Tell me where you live.
ME	I don't know if I can do that.
MYRA	Tell me.
ME	I don't know, Myra.
MYRA	Tell me *now*.
ME	OK OK I'll tell you. I live at

then I pressed the
button on the phone to make the line dead. I could say we
got cut off and it was nothing to do with me. I let the receiver
hang at the side of the phone, purring on the carpet so she
couldn't call back while I ran upstairs. I leaned over the sink
and brushed my teeth hard till the spit went dark pink,
pressing the brush into the gum to punish myself enough so
god would let Myra leave me alone. All the time I was muttering through the bristles staining the basin with drips.

> she doesn't know my address
> she doesn't know my address

I've been afraid of Myra ever since I remember. She and my
mother/ her mother were pregnant at the same time. She
could have been my mother. I think about that if I feel hard
done by, making myself grateful for small mercies. Myra's
baby died. I didn't. Maybe that was why she hit me so much.
I don't know. Hands like shovels. Myra left marks. None of
them show.

I rinsed the sink and waited for a while, not knowing what
to do next. After a while I came downstairs to pace up and
down on the edge of the rug. I thought about going out but
there was nowhere I could think of to go. Besides, I wanted
to be in possession of the livingroom if anything happened.
The phone only works one way.

The twisty road outside was orange under the streetlamps,
shiny with rain. Leaves like little bits of peel in unset
marmalade. Gangs of kids roared past the end of the lane,
screaming. I sat in the armchair till my knees went pale blue.

> she doesn't know my address
> she doesn't know my address

The room filled with dark like settling dust.

I was getting catatonic when the knocking came. Knocking and a noise like a key in the lock. I listened to my own breathing. The knocking came again: flesh on wood, scratching. The letterbox was rattling.

ANSWER THE DOOR

Everything was still for a long moment. Then the door shook and thudded heavily once or twice like something huge was butting against it from the outside. It creaked as though it was splintering.

I KNOW YOU'RE IN THERE

Like a fish on a line, I drew towards the inside door. I could hear the outside door rattle louder the nearer I got, shaking, billowing inwards with the force of the shovel hands. But I kept going. The lock made ice-burns on my fingers. But I submit, I submit. I always do. I turned the key and stood back.

Myra whirled in from the black outside, like a dervish: her hair completely grey. I had to look twice but it was Myra all right. Older. I had never thought to see Myra looking older. Her makeup had run into coaldust triangles while she had been waiting outside in the howling gale and the rain for someone to come and let her in. Her nose was red as a bitten thumb.

WHERE THE HELL HAVE YOU BEEN?

The voice was just the same. Then it softened a little.
   I've been at this door for ages. Ages. You've no idea what's been running through my head.

She was right: I hadn't. But I was ashamed because I hadn't answered and for trying to hide. I was ashamed because she looked so old. I would have kept her out if I could. Her hands were chapped and she wasn't wearing gloves. There was a sudden suck of air as I hauled the outer door shut so the leaves in the porch zoomed up at our faces like bats. I could hardly believe what I was doing. I was taking Myra into my house. I watched myself incredulously, knowing with a terrible sinking of heart it could only get worse.

She looks horrible when I put on the light. I imagine I do too. Blood sisters. Sisters grimm.

This is it, she says, standing in the middle of the thread-bare rug. You've cleared all the bloody junk out of it anyway.
I don't know what she's talking about. Then I never did. When I point at one of the sheet-covered chairs, she sits, smiles, looks up.
This is all right. This is fine.
I remember I'm scared and go through to the kitchen saying I have to make tea. She shouts she's not thirsty, missing the point of why I need to get away, but she stays put while I barge about the kitchen dropping cups and spoons, spilling milk powder. I have to come to terms with this. I have to speak to her. This is my sister for christsake. My sister.

My sister looks at me over the tea, warming her chipped hands, saying things that don't register too well. The tea squirms in my throat when I swallow. My sister is here in the livingroom. *Myra.*

Myra is twenty-three years older than me. Nearly fifty. She looks older, runnels of dripping mascara on her cheeks and this grey hair. She looks crazy. I laugh when I think that and she smiles back at me, mistaking it as a gesture of friendship. She relaxes some more.

Ma's fruit bowl. I forgot you had it. You've cleared the stuff out. Hellish stuff. The fuses and that. Mind yon plastic flowers she liked? The bullrushes? Jesus eh?

I remember she drinks a good deal and wonder if that's the

reason for the slurring, the difficulty of making sense of what she's trying to say. She sounds as though she's had a stroke. Maybe she has. I know nothing about my own sister. She says *you know?* as she speaks and I lie. I nod and nod but I don't know anything. I get the gin. Myra notices there isn't much left. I swill it fast and go back for something else. I pour two big glasses of sherry and sit the rest where it's handy.

We clink glasses. CHEERS we say. Cheers. Christ.

The sherry tastes like sugar water but serves the purpose. We are veering into the difficult territory of How Things Are.
Little dust clouds puff in an aureole round her head as Myra eases back into the chair. I know it's coming.
　So, she says. How Are Things?
　Fine, I say. Too quick.
　She says, No how are you really. *Really* is what I mean. *Really.*
I shake my head and look at the sherry. The glass isn't clean.
　She says, No I mean it tell me I mean it right enough you know?
There's a silence but for Myra sniffing, her nose on the thaw.
　No but somebody died, she says. Somebody says to me somebody died and you were sick. Did you try to do yourself in or what? Who died?
I slump. But this has to be gone through. She is here and I am here and I can't think how to make the question go away.

　So who died?
　A man I was living with. I wave my arm expansively. This is his house.
　This is a nice place, she says, casting a watery eye round the ruins of old furniture and the sheets.
I have to control the urge to throw back my head and guffaw like a drain. Sherry shoots up my nose and makes me choke. I'm almost sick with holding it down.
　How did you get it? she says, oblivious.
　It wasn't easy, I say. I had no entitlement. He was married

62

and the separation wasn't finalised. But his wife was kind enough to let me have all this crap she didn't want.

Alcohol fumes smart my eyes. I've had more to drink than I thought. I am not being careful.

Married, she says, as though it explains everything. Married man. HAH!

He asked for a big place so the kids could come. There are two bedrooms upstairs.

Kids, christ! Kids! Bloody like the thing eh? Typical.

I think for a minute but I don't know what it is that's typical. I have to say something. I say, No, it was OK. Everything was OK to start with. We lived in my place for a while and everything was OK. Then we came here.

Where from? she says, raking in her bag. Her nose is running now.

Och, Myra it goes on forever.

This cheery intonation I get when I'm well on: something to do with a race memory of New Year. I look into the sherry glass and try to stop my mouth going any further.

The cottage was tiny but cheap. There was a bus stop right outside the door and people with no sense used to look in while they were waiting for the bus, as though I was TV. But it also meant travel: buses stopping and starting right outside my door for whenever I needed to go somewhere. It made me feel free. I papered every wall myself and built shelves, wired my own plugs and painted the place fresh. A kind of damp smell hung on in the kitchen but it was my own place, my home now. Paul helped move my things. The parting wasn't bitter. We wanted to be civilised and polite. Unexplained bouts of weeping disturbed the quiet some evenings but I figured they were good signs. Everybody needs to cry now and then. I was there less than six months when Michael phoned his two word call.

She knows.

He moved in the same night with three carrier bags. There was nowhere else for him to go. He missed the kids but we were OK. Some nights we'd stay awake right through on the pleasure of holding the other warm body in the dark we never expected would be there. We got up red-eyed for work to go to the same place in the same car, came home together at night. When we washed the dishes, we'd watch our reflections in the night-blacked window, kissing.

One night, he got out of bed and didn't come back for a while. It was 2am. I got uneasy about it. I found him in the kitchenette, right at the back of the cottage, turning lilac in the cold. He was kneeling on the concrete looking at something. I kneeled down too and tried to see what it was. There was a mushroom growing out of the skirting. LOOK he said, LOOK. We didn't know what to think. I poked it with a fork and it broke off. We went back to bed and tried to forget about it.

sometin
presenti
tell us tc
it's too l
ignore tl
sometim
that feel
deja

We were in the kitchen cooking: I was throwing spaghetti onto the roughcast to see if it was ready while he was stirring sauce. The spaghetti landed awkwardly and I saw another mushroom right next to where it had settled on the wall. LOOK I said and we both looked again. This one was more securely attached. It didn't break first time so Michael got a knife and cut it away from the side of the window. It left a little pink trail like anaemic blood where it had been growing. After a month there were little shoots all along the hallway. Mould drew lines round the tops of walls and baby mushrooms appeared overnight. I wouldn't let him touch them because I thought they were dangerous or something. I didn't know where they were coming from and preferred just to let them alone in case. In case. Maybe I thought they would go away if we pretended hard enough. Every so often, I would find him in the hall or the kitchen, peering down and scratching with a penknife, then trying to hide it when he saw me coming. I would hear him in the bathroom, running the taps and washing his hands. He got a book from the library and read up about mushrooms.

Dry rot, he said, matter-of-factly.

Dry rot. He gave me the book so I could read about it too. It was more sinister than the name. The house was being eaten from the inside by this thing. The spores could pass though concrete and plaster and multiplied by the thousand thousand as we slept. They could take over the whole structure if they wanted. I lay awake at night wondering what was going on out there in the hall while we were in our beds. The estimates for fixing it were unbelievable. I started having trouble sleeping. I avoided looking at the walls or skirting during the day.

Meantime Michael's council application paid off. The place was too big but he took it. It was cheerful, bright, full of windows. Yellow walls and white woodwork. It was important he had his own place so he needn't feel dependant. Besides I didn't want anyone staying with me out of necessity. People gave us bits of things to fill it with. We shipped in the clothes from the cottage during the night, away from the silent spores, the creeping red clouds. We set down rugs and covered the chairs with sheets to hide the burst seams and chipped frames. We hung ancient curtains held together with stour. I cooked chicken in his oven and we ate it with too much wine, setting our lives to rights. The cottage could be fixed while I stayed here, then I'd go back to my own home. When he came to me or I to him, it would be from choice. It was very civilised. The magazines would have approved like hell. We could afford civilised decisions now: do things we'd always wanted to. Everything was going to be all right. Reckless, we booked a holiday we couldn't afford in Spain. Warm open air, the sun. The beach. Swimming pools. We could deal with the cottage when we got back. We would be rested. We would be able to think clearly. The money would turn up. His stars said so.

> Money has been tight but sunshine summer
> brings relief you never thought possible. Some-
> thing new is opening up for you and your
> partner. Your worries may soon be a thing of the

distant past. Splash out and don't fight shy of the change:it may just be for the better!

Want any more of this?
A woman with grey hair offers me a bottle. Myra. She pours me something and I swill it back and choke. Whisky. She's brought her own bottle. Myra gurgles away the last of hers and pours a fresh one.
Married men, she says and I get cold all over.
I look up at this woman and try to see someone who gave me a Mickey Mouse toy that made me so excited I was sick. All I see is a woman with grey hair.
She leans forward chummily and says, So this is your place now, eh?
I think about the cottage crumbling. I look round the yellow walls and white woodwork, the strings of dust trailing in the corners.
Yes, this is all mine.
How did you get it? she says, impressed again.
Mr Dick pops uninvited into my head, his face spread and too close, like a reflection in a doorknob.

We're bending over backwards, Miss Stone; you should realise that. Strictly speaking, you're breaking and entering every night. Mrs. Fisher's lawyers are quite right when they say that. You have no right to the keys, Miss Stone. You don't seem to realise the delicacy of the situation. You miss the point. We're already being generous under tremendous strain.

I clutch my hand tighter round the glass.
Long story, I say.
Married men, Myra says. Her eyes close gently.

Her words have been slurring more. I leave my glass to one side and try to stand upright without disturbing her. She can

66

do terrible things when she's drunk. I'm only half-way upright when a sudden hiccup catches me out. The hiccup has caught her off guard. She sits uprught, momentarily terrified then shouts right in my ear.

What about your mother you callous bitch? Never gret for your mother. And starts to cry.

I yell something about making tea and run like hell to the kitchen. There's a call box at the end of the road. I rack my brain, listening to the awful sounds of Myra weeping next door and come up with Paul. There is no-one else who knows what I mean when I use the word *Myra*. When I say *Myra is in the house and you have to help me.* I need to trade on old times.

I'm just putting the kettle on, I shout to cover the sound of the key turning in the back door. The freezing cold comes and touches me while I find change in the kitchen drawer and run like hell to the callbox, hoping. It has no door and smells bad and almost never works. Tonight it does. It purrs when I lift it to my face, the grille oily from other people's breath. The wind buffets the sides of the box as I dial and forget, redial and forget. It's almost midnight but I have to call. It rings and rings at the other side, the wind howling so loud I clutch the receiver and fret I won't hear when he answers. Then he does. Just the same voice, Paul's voice, natural as pain for seven years. He's laid back, relaxed in his own home that used to be where I lived.

PAUL   Hi. Who's calling?
ME   Paul?
PAUL   Yes. Who's speaking?
ME   It's OK, it's just me. It's me, Paul. Look, I know it's late but can you speak to me just speak to me I'm scared I'm frightened and there's nobody else to call please can I.
PAUL   Listen. [He sounds different now. As if he's been conned] Listen to me. Just calm down. What do you want?
ME   Sorry. I was getting hysterical.

I think I'm going to cry and have to bite my lip hard while he waits sighing at the end of the line. I get in again fast before he thinks I'm crazy or something. I play my ace.

ME   Myra's here.
PAUL   [Long silence]
ME   Paul? Myra's here.
PAUL   I know. She phoned and asked for your address.
ME   [Nothing. I think I'm going to implode.]
PAUL   I had to do something to get her off the line. I have people here. I don't want her phoning me. Tell her not to do it again.
ME   But she's here in my house.
PAUL   So?
ME   [The whine starts. It's embarrassing but since it's started I hope it might make him guilty.] I'm scared. Can you come round and do something?
PAUL   O for goodness' sake. What do you expect me to do?
ME   [This is a good question and has me floored. I sag against the heaving side of the callbox and whisper.] Help me.
PAUL   Look. I have people here. People.
ME   What will I do?
PAUL   I have people here. [Silence] People. Don't you understand? [Big sigh] O for christsake

There was a choking sound and the phone trailed into a line of dots. It took a minute or two before I could admit Paul hung up on me then I slid further down the booth, trying to get out of knowing. The yellow square of my kitchen window flickered and I knew Myra was moving around in there. Looking for me. So I walked back to the house. I didn't stumble once. No matter how often I think I can't stand it any more, I always do. There is no alternative. I don't fall, I don't foam at the mouth, faint, collapse or die. It's the same for all of us. You can't get out of the inside of your own head. Something keeps you going. Something always does. I went back to the house and Myra. On my own.

This Is The Way Things Are Now.

The clock says 12.44.
Tomorrow is Tuesday.
I try to think what it means. Tuesday. The second day of the
working week. This is a joke but I don't laugh much. I'm
also wrong. 12.45. The green display on the stereo says it
over and over while I count. It's Tuesday today. The
numbers flicker and change silently.

*Two women come in bathing suits, closer by de-
grees.*

*A whale hump of backbone over someone lying on
the tiles: the shape of two men, kissing. Only one
man moves. The arms and faces of other people slip
past. Vomit touches the back of my throat.*

> *jesus*
> *jesus*
> *jesu*

*Dutch or German. A language I don't know. They
circle the man on the tiles. His fingers channel
floods.*

*A white truck skids too close to the side of the pool
and a child starts howling. Women recede into the
crowd, their faces yellow: canary pale under the
leather tan.*

*Two men run from the white truck door. They lift
the shape of a man, its limbs slack. Relax. A hand on*

my shoulder and my tongue clots with sand. Inside the truck, the leather seat hot under my thigh. The metal clatter of locks.

Outside, red and purple flowers swim over the window, blurring with speed, the trembling under the tyres. Gears jar and lurch the flowers away. A siren wails.

ooo

The alarm.
I ricochet upright before I realise that's all it is.

Tuesday Morning.
I have to go to work.
I have to go to work because
        1. it will be warmer than here;
        2. it brings home the bacon;
        3. there will be people.

I wrap up in two layers of clothes against the frost.

Myra never ate breakfast, just black coffee. I used to copy her because I thought it was very sophisticated. My mother would shout YOU NEED BREAKFAST AT YOUR AGE but I left her to have toast alone and went to school empty and light.

The morning after Myra came, I remembered but asked what she'd like out of thinking I was supposed to. Maybe she'd changed.
    You know I don't eat stuff in the morning, she said. Just the same. Very chirpy.
Just the same.

We shared black coffee then walked up to the stop, knee-deep in mist.

Christ what time is it? she said.
Just after seven. I told her about the buses and how I had to leave early.
Christ, she said.
We kept our ears lively since the fog was too thick for looking. Her nose, still crimson from the night before, dripped onto the concrete. She coughed, wiping the wet away with the bare hand before she squinted out at me from the corner of a bloodshot eye.

Will I not come again?
My stomach started looping.
Do you not want me to come again? Do you think -
but she didn't finish the sentence, just let it hang there broken at the end with nothing to come and fill the void. I thought I could hear ticking though neither of us had a watch and there was no clock. Maybe water was dripping from the guttering on top of the shelter. We were out in the middle of nowhere in particular standing in a perspex shelter, for christsake. There was no clock but something was ticking. She wiped her nose again and the rims of her eyes went shiny.
I'm your sister.

I looked at the pavement in case she started crying. The last time I saw Myra cry was the time my mother wouldn't let her go out with an Italian waiter. She had on this big dirndl skirt and hoop earrings, the mascara making tiger stripes through the orange panstick. She hit my mother and went out anyway. I was five. I didn't know what to say then either.
Sister.
She wasn't going to let it go.
A lump fought in my throat like a spider coming up through sand. I can never keep my mouth shut.
Yes. Aye, sure. Come again if you need to. But it's not easy for me, Myra. There's too much..stuff. Too much bad stuff

71

from before. I don't even know if you listen to me. I don't know if we can just -

I'll not come if you don't want.

She sniffed. Her mouth was all set and I couldn't stand it.

No. Don't do that if you need to come. You can come again. It's just that we don't have much -

I'm not coming where I'm not wanted.

She turned sideways, peering uselessly into the distance. The fog was choking.

No, I said through my teeth. No. You are after all. You are. I couldn't say what she was. Just couldn't get my mouth round *sister*.

The bus was coming. I waved it down in case he missed us: just these two black shapes in the mist. The noise of the brakes like chalk down a board. She gathered her coat up tight and went forward but the minute she lifted her foot to the platform something hurt me. Something of me was attached and pulling with her though I didn't want it to. She was walking on inside, waving with her face changing and trying to be cheery. The bus started drawing away.

I'm sorry Myra.

I whispered watching the bus disappear into the fog.

I'm sorry. I always do the wrong thing.

christ

8.15. Daydreaming and forgot the time. I run but the car isn't there. The women will be late and will have been cursing me all the road in. Serves me right.

ooo

Cairdwell Secondary is in the middle of nowhere. It takes over an hour on the bus then another mile on foot. That's a lot of bother for something you don't want to do in the first place but I do it all the same. The mural has been defaced:

72

arrows through the kids' heads and FIONA LOVES GONZO, the
Os shaped like coffins. I get as far as lunchtime before a
chunk of a boy with a moustache brings a billet doux on
pink paper. Mr Peach would like to see me in his office.
Last time Mr Peach sent for me was almost a month ago.
Nearly a whole cycle of the moon. I tried to be on my guard
as an extra precaution, even though he was trying hard to
be a good egg/ Mr Reasonable/ a real sweetie-pie. I thought
I'd stay cautious Just In Case. I hadn't a clue.
He sat me down and said looked serious. Then he coughed
and said

  We're thinking of having a Service for Mr Fisher.
I knew there was a right answer to this but I didn't know
what it was. He had ink on his finger, just above his wedding
ring.

I said, It's nice of you to ask me. I appreciate being asked.
He wiped his nose and nodded so I knew it was the right
answer. I was supposed to appreciate being asked. But I was
still cautious: personal questions don't belong where people
work so I knew I had to look out for the hidden agenda. I
thought I was being so careful.

  We could have readings from the bible, pieces of music,
he said, warming up now. The Reverend Dogcollar might
say a few words.

  Yes, I said. Why not?

  He smiled then thought better of it, looked me deep in the
eye and lowered his voice.

  Mrs Fisher will have to be invited. Of course.

The *of course* was thoughtful but unnecessary. I wanted to
be civilised and polite. I had a thing about being civilised and
polite: it would have driven me crazy for anyone to think I
was petty-minded or spiteful.

  Yes of course, of course Mrs Fisher should be there of
course.
I appreciated being asked. This was my workplace. It made
me warm to be so valued. Of course of course of course. He

73

twisted his ring and rubbed off the ink-stain. It was all settled.

I forgot I always expect too much.
I forgot I always do the wrong thing.

ooo

The dolly on the door of the Ladies' sports green felt-tip breasts: they're new. The only thing that is. Inside, the same group of regulars apply the same lipstick they apply every lunchtime. I carry a stick of flesh-coloured make-up to blot out the circles under my eyes. I do this several times a day but usually in my room. Doing it here makes me feel conspicuous but I do it anyway. The woman at the nearside sink drops a used paper towel into the wastebin and pats her hair, coming too close. When I lift my head she's pushing out her lower lip and winding up an endless stick of sugar pink. Smile, she chirps. It might never happen.

Mr Peach looks distraught when I open the door. This is his usual expression so I don't take too much from it. He tells me to sit and adjusts his specs: nervous habit. Optional extras include knitting of fingers and gazing at the blotter, little anxious ticks that put the burden of soothing on whoever has to watch them. Today he does the works. I know I don't want to play this game.

BOSS	You're not looking well.
EMPLOYEE	....
BOSS	You know why I asked you here?
EMPLOYEE	....
BOSS	[Uncertainly] You do know why I asked you here?
EMPLOYEE	....
BOSS	This is all since the service for Mr Fisher, isn't it?
EMPLOYEE	....

74

BOSS	You sent the Reverend Dogcollar a letter.
EMPLOYEE	....
BOSS	I think you show an unrealistic attitude. You, if anyone, should have been realistic.
EMPLOYEE	Oh? [Dammit. He knew this one would get me. I can't keep silent much longer.]
BOSS	You are a realist, aren't you? I thought you were.
EMPLOYEE	[Dammit] You miss the point.
BOSS	I thought you were a realist but you haven't been very realistic about this.
EMPLOYEE	I don't think what happened at that service had anything to do with realism. Quite the reverse. I think it was in terrible taste.
BOSS	I don't see what you mean. I don't see that at all. You show an unrealistic attitude. It was a tricky situation. You knew that. I explained to you at the time. I thought you understood. Now how are you really?

The shift of ground was clever. I get docile with confusion.

BOSS	How are you coping? I want you to know nobody thinks you're going off your head. And you should try to cheer up.
EMPLOYEE	What?
BOSS	Try to cheer up. It upsets me to think you aren't happy. It upsets me to see you like this. You float past in the corridor and I never see you smile.
EMPLOYEE	I'm sorry about that. It's nothing personal.
BOSS	Yes. No-one is against you. You'll antagonise people if you don't make an effort.
EMPLOYEE	Yes.
BOSS	Smile then. I want you to look happy. We all do. Give us a smile.

He opens the door for me on the way out. I keep my head down past the hideous mural of the family shot through with arrows, listening to my shoes on the tile. Coffee and salami, warm pastry waft out of the staffroom, scents of food that get me so I don't know what I'm doing any more. I stand in the corridor and start to cry. Dammit dammit. Holding my hand up to my face to hide the swollen nose *vanity, vanity*, I go to the office and ask to go home. I don't wait for the answer. Just run like hell.

ooo

Slats are missing off the back fence. Kids take them to make bonfires. Also the back door is stiff and takes three goes to shove open, like it's rusting over. I should try to use it more often. The minute I get in the kids start yelling: a high, dog-whine that will go on all night. I got fed-up with it once and went out with a prepared speech - the boy who cried wolf and all that. There were about eight little to middling kids. The smallest was the one doing the howling, his head tilted up and hitting the grass verge with a big stick. I did the whole speech without one of them looking in my direction. After I went away the howling got worse and about one in the morning bricks started hitting the back door. Now I just pull the curtains and switch on the TV.

Opening a new bottle can't be rushed. It takes most of my Saturday pay: all those tedious hours of smoke and other peoples' cash, going home reeking of coins and nicotine. I take my time breaking the seal, feeling it crack and snap under my hand, twisting the metal. So thin you can feel the thread of the glass ripple through. The pink tissue is pretty. The gin comes out with an animal sound, like something lapping up milk.

No magazine. Gin *and* a magazine would make me spoilt. Tonight I tell my own future. The tarot cards live in a box beneath the settee. Paul bought me these cards one Christmas. I gave him a knife. He said knives as presents were unlucky and gave me a silver coin. To stop the knife severing the friendship he said.

I spread the cards and choose, radiate six like sun rays on the carpet then flex my fingers and sigh. As soon as they're chosen they become certainties.

_p

> The first is the Hanged Man, inverted. Caught by his heel to the sky, hair rising to the ground. He lifts and settles in the draught from under the door.
> The Empress. A woman in possession of what is rightfully hers.
> The Wheel of Fortune, inverse. Six spokes and a twin-pillared frame: an ape, a dog and a dragon clasp the revolving wheel.

I wait a moment before turning the fourth: The Fool.

The floor is littered with messages I can't read.
There is no armour against the arbitrariness of things. Not suspicion, not fear. There is no way to predict, divine or escape. The only certainty is that there is no certainty. Suspicion is never enough.

I pour another drink and turn up the TV. The wall thumps and my neighbour's little girl screams.

ooo

The day of the service was overcast but warm. I laid out my clothes like a little girl, smoothing the seams neat. Perfume, ear-rings, ring. Roses and lily-of-the-valley. When the bell for assembly rang I was ready, hands stiff on the buttons of my new black jacket, fussing the bow of the blouse. I couldn't get rid of the smile: it was stuck like one of those threats people make to kids about the wind changing etc etc. So I paced up and down in my room, waiting with this aching face.

When David came we walked across the tarmac to the hall without touching. He was trying to be collected and not look as though he was here specifically for me. The hall doors were closing when we shuffled in at the back, late. At the front there was a black lectern with flowers. Everyone stood up. The minister raised his hands and held them outstretched, looking us in the corporate eye.

It didn't make sense to begin with. I couldn't place the accent: the vowel sounds in no pattern I could recognise or anticipate. Like a badly-dubbed movie. Looking didn't help: his face was the colour of a baked bean with the sauce washed off. I looked at the flowers round the lectern instead and caught sight of Norma Fisher in the front row. I almost waved. But the Rev must have known I wasn't paying attention. He raised his voice.

WE ARE HERE TODAY TO MOURN THE LOSS OF A DEAR COLLEAGUE

The unmistakable air of someone drawing events to a close. He stretched the arms out again and made a longer and more intense pause than usual. The sun filled up in the overhead windows and outlined the white hair with silver. I thought we were home and dry.

THIS SERVICE HAS BEEN ONE OF
JOY AND CELEBRATION AS
WELL AS SORROW

                         I noticed he rolled his eyes
                          unpleasantly

THOUGH THE SORROW IS
UPPERMOST IN OUR HEARTS. AS
WE CLOSE, LET US THINK OF
WHAT MICHAEL FISHER
BROUGHT TO OUR LIVES. BUT
MORE ESPECIALLY IN THESE
MOMENTS OF SILENCE

                          and his arms began to
                          stretch out towards the front
                          rows

EXTEND OUR SYMPATHIES, OUR
HEARTS AND OUR LOVE

> the arms stretching further
> like Jesus commanding
> Lazarus

ESPECIALLY OUR LOVE

> a split-second awareness that
> something terrible was about
> to about to

TO HIS WIFE AND FAMILY   happen

Half-way into the silence for Norma Fisher, my arms were
weightless. The rest came piecemeal as the moral started to
compute.

1. The Rev Dogsbody had chosen this service to perform a
   miracle.
2. He'd run time backwards, cleansed, absolved and got rid
   of the ground-in stain.
3. And the stain was me.
I didn't exist. The miracle had wiped me out.

The first symptom of non-existence is weightlessness.
The second is singing in the ears, a quiet acceptance of the
unreality of all things. Then the third takes over in earnest.
The third is shaking.

David had hold of my arm and we were walking too fast
down the white corridor, the mural on the stairs. Something
in my mouth, gagging with the salt taste. Thick salt bands
across my mouth were Sean's fingers. I could hear breath in
my ears, gagging with the salt taste and someone yelling.

I knew it couldn't be me.
I didn't exist.
The miracle had wiped me out.

The white truck doors, clatter of metal.
I can't feel my arms
        jesus
        jesus say there's nothing wrong say
        jesus

They tell me to wait and I hear something thumping, flesh
against flesh behind the closed door. I retch but nothing
comes.

        jesus
        jesus

A boy appears.
He speaks English, he tells me. English.
Heavy inflections on words I should recognise from a pale
boy mouth, brown eyes still at the core. The boy runs out of
words.

I wait for someone else to speak. No-one does.
I speak but no-one understands.

Doctors whisper and push the boy forward. Behind his
back, the nurse testing a needle as
the boy's mouth opens, fracturing on unfamiliar syllables

                What was his name?

The needle glints
and there is someone

          screaming

The rug is hard under my hip, my face brittle. Bits of broken glass on the carpet shimmer through the dark. The arm I've been sleeping on is completely numb.

I get up awkwardly, rubbing the arm. Something is out of place: subtle changes in the position of the furniture, the occasional slip from three dimensions to two. 3.20. I switch off the TV whistling blind in the corner and hobble upstairs for the pill bottle. A moan from next door when I open the bedroom door. Maybe she hears me, turning in her sleep. I lie stroking the wall till my arm is numb again.

ooo

Wednesday Morning.
The clock ticks too loud. It's been too loud for ages but I haven't done anything about it, just lain here letting it wear my teeth down to the dentine. I lie like a sack of waterlogged sand. It should be an easy thing, a simple thing to get out of bed and go to work. People do it every day. But some days I get too heavy to move. A piece of sky outside. I know I won't go to work.

Jesus.

I can't think how I fell into this unProtestant habit. I used to be so conscientious. I used to be so *good* all the time.
[where good = productive/hardworking/wouldn't say boo]
I was a good student: straight passes down the line. First year probationer taking home reams of paper, planning courses and schemes for kids that weren't my own. People made jokes, I was so eager to please. That's how good I used to be.
                    [where good = value for money]

I was very good at my mother's funeral though largely by default.

81

[where **good** = not putting anyone out by feeling too much, blank, unobtrusive]

I was very good because I didn't believe she was dead. I thought she was only pretending to get attention and would jump out of the box later and laugh at me for being a sap if I cried (see footnote*). So I sat looking expectantly at the dais ringed by red curtains, waiting for the coffin to do something. After a while it slipped backwards and the curtains shut. I knew it was over because people started coming to shake my hand. But I was remarkably good. Didn't spill a drop.

Michael's was my first burial. I kept my eye on the coffin the whole time just in case. Sean came up afterwards and held my arm to make me walk. I managed. I was tasteful because I wanted people's approval. Good girls reap rewards.

[where **good** = neat, acting in a credit-worthy manner]
I knew the routine. Like everybody, I wanted to be loved.

First day back this term I wore a dress. I was neat. I handed in his music room keys and scored his name off the staff list with a single black line. I was discreet. I knew the whole thing was just a matter of lasting out. If I was a good [ie **patient, thoughtful, uncomplaining**] girl long enough I would reap the reward. I didn't go into specifics at the time about what the reward would be. Maybe I really believed I could magic him back to

o yes
when I was good I was very very good but
but
there was more going on below the surface.
There always is. There is always more to come.

The smiling could only be accomplished by grinding my teeth. I woke every morning and there was still no sign of the

---

* Love/Emotion = embarrassment: Scots equation. Exceptions are when roaring drunk or watching football. Men do rather better out of this loophole.

prize. I resented these mornings. They nursed a grudge bigger than I knew how to control. I reined myself in with fake scripture. God isn't fooled by mercenary goodness I told myself and went back to manic smiling.

Look
all I wanted to be was civilised and polite. I wanted to be no trouble. I wanted to be brave and discreet. This had to be the final stage of the endurance test and all I had to do was last out. I thought I was Bunyan's Pilgrim and Dorothy in the Wizard of Oz. But the lasting out was terrible. I made appointments with the doctor and he gave me pills to tide me over when I got anxious. I got anxious when they didn't tide me over into anything different. He gave me more pills. I kept going to work. I was no nearer Kansas or the Celestial City. Then

I started smelling Michael's aftershave in the middle of the night. I would go to bed and there it was, in a cloud all round my head. I thought if I could smell his aftershave he must be around somewhere. I saw him in cars, across the street, in buses, roaring past on strange motorbikes, drifting by the glass panel of my classroom door. I read his horoscope. How could he be having a difficult phase with money if he was dead? Of course he wasn't *dead*: just hiding. At night I sunk my face into his clothes and howled at the cloth. A magazine article said it was fairly common and not as unhealthy as you'd think. Then I would go to bed and wait for the slow seep of aftershave through the ether. I knew he wasn't just a carcass liquefying in a wooden box but an invisible presence hovering in a cloud of Aramis above my bed. I also suspected I was lying. When I found the bottle, tipped on its side and leaking along the rim I knew for sure. I had put it there myself ages ago so I could reach for it and smell his neck when I wanted to feel like hell in the middle of the night. Then I must have knocked it over and been too wilful to admit to what it was later. My own duplicity shocked me. I held onto the bottle for a week or so then threw it out.

My mother was right. I have no common sense. I don't know a damn thing worth knowing.

THE CHURCH	THE MARRIED
THE LAW	WHAT'S WHAT

I haven't a clue.

The clock ticks too loud while I lie still, shrinking.

Please god make boulders crash through the roof. In three or four days when the Health Visitor comes she will find only mashed remains, marrowbone jelly oozing between the shards like bitumen. *Well*, she'll say, *We're not doing so well today, are we?* It's too cold. The hairs on my legs are stiff. I shiver and wish the phone would ring.

Needing people yet being afraid of them is wearing me out. I struggle with the paradox all the time and can't resolve it. When people visit I am distraught trying to look as if I can cope. At work I never speak but I want to be spoken to. If anyone does I get anxious and stammer. I'm scared of the phone yet I want it to ring.

ooo

Surprise!
Ellen rushes to the door in an apron and slippers. The apron draws attention to my terrible timing. Lunchtime.
    Well stranger! Day off?
I create diversion out of her lilac rinse and she gets embarrassed, not sure if it suits her. When she pats her hair I notice the smear of tomato paste on the side of her hand and know what's coming next.

Well, she says, recovered from the diversion in record

time. Well. I'm just having a spot of lunch, will you join me?

Ellen is always having a spot of lunch/ supper/ a little something when I call. She thinks food is medicine. Marianne sent a picture of herself already fattening on hamburgers and rootbeer and Ellen cried because she looked peaky. Ellen's cat is gargantuan. It frightens dogs. For Ellen, food is love. We stand in the hall of this big house on the hill, me with my terrible timing and Ellen with her need to feed. The house is full of the smell of cooking.

HEALTH UPDATE: ULTIMATE DIET

By this time, not eating has become so rewarding you won't want to stop. And who can blame you? But avoiding food is harder than you'd think. Repeated refusing starts to look rude and thoughtless. You know it's important they shouldn't see the deliberateness of your choice and indeed, sometimes it's hard not to develop a degree of paranoia in view of how persistent some people can be! You think they want to feed you as part of a conspiracy of fatness to undermine your hard-won control. Don't be afraid to develop a list of ingenious lies to sidestep their frequent assaults: say you've just eaten/ aren't too hungry right now/ feel squeamish today/ had a big breakfast/ are meeting someone later etc. Scrutinise their faces to see if they will leave you alone or persist. If they persist, avoid them in future. I must warn you however that in spite of the denials, you want. The taste and texture of food obsesses. You buy magazines on the strength of the recipes, read menus in restaurant windows. Overheard conversations about food become as illicitly exciting as the sound of a couple screwing in the room next door. Allow nibbles of biscuit, the odd cracker or piece of fruit. Feel the tension in your stomach after even the lightest meal as a warning. Drink endlessly to bulk away the craving. You know it'll all be worth it in the end.

Ellen stands there in the doorway.

I'm just having a spot of lunch, will you join me? she says, her eyes searching for clues.

Lovely, I say. I'm starving.

It isn't even a joke.

We eat   baked potatoes with butter
             cauliflower cheese
             farmhouse bread with butter
             chocolate cake with extra cream
             shortbread and coffee

jesus

Afterwards I sit on Ellen's posh cream velour sofa with another coffee, stomach boggling with calories. Ellen smiles like a split melon under the lilac rinse while the pain gets worse.

You don't think the pattern's too young for me?

No, it's lovely. Lovely colour.

I couldn't care less about the bloody wool but I keep going, drinking more coffee, trying to sit still. It's important to keep drinking so the next part's easier. We do knitting, prices, the nights are fair drawing in and letters from Marianne. When I think I'm going to explode with fluid, I get up and go to the toilet.

I know exactly what to do.

I learned this about a month ago when Sam came, just before he went to college. We went out on his bike then to Sean's. The whole family were downstairs and he was baking at almost midnight. The house full of the smell of hot dough and the kids up at the table with crayons. It was like something out of the Waltons. Sean brought tea and a tray with seven of the fresh rolls, butter, chocolate biscuits. I could have said it was too late for me to eat or I get indigestion this time of night - any one of a number of plausible things from the repertoire. But I didn't. I was watching Sean break one of the rolls with his hands, the crust shearing along the top and sides, flaking onto the tablecover. He held half out in one palm.

Take it, he nodded at the butter. Take it.

It was still warm. I ate four of the rolls and three biscuits before I knew what I was doing. When Sam took me home I shambled through farewells thinking what to do about the tightness in my chest: I barely waved. The minute the bike

86

was out of sight I rushed like hell inside straight upstairs to
the mirror to check my face for signs of swelling. What's
more, I could see them. I turned the taps to full pressure and
checked again. There was only one thing to do.
I swallowed my hand up to the wrist.

The first time was kind of messy. Now I'm better.
I go into Ellen's bathroom and throw up silently for ten
minutes.
Every girl has her emergency measures. This just happens to
be mine.

The livingroom is soft-focus in the glow from the fire when
I emerge. My head thumping, my throat raw and my eyes
still watering, I sit on Ellen's clean sofa and make smalltalk.
My mouth feels rinsed with paintstripper and sometimes my
gums bleed. Digestive acids eat tooth-enamel. But I make
smalltalk and Ellen knits. I have another coffee before I
leave.

ooo

The livingroom rug is covered with meaningless bits of
cloth.
I'm in no mood. Dressmaking is not as rewarding as they'd
have you believe. Gin tastes sweet and bitter at the same
time, stripping down in clean lines, blooming like an acid
flower in the pit of my stomach. I top up the glass till it's
seeping. If I get drunk enough, I won't go to work tomorrow
either. This is cheering and helps me through another
mouthful.

> Do not
> operate machinery
> Avoid alcohol

Red and yellow pills: two thirds of a traffic light. The red
ones come in push-through foil packs like contraceptives.

Little touch of humour. HA HA Dr Stead. Very funny. He prescribes only a week's worth at a time in case. In case my arse. Just another control technique.

Dear Marianne,
I went to see your mother today and she's fine. I'm fine too. We're all fine. I'm so fine I'm writing you this. Work is not fine but I mustn't be greedy. The Whitewater rafting card came. It looks terrible.

Marianne likes all that stuff. Guides and Brownies from an early age. She knows how to light fires with old birds' nests, etc. Her idea of a good time is going somewhere remote and inconvenient to get really uncomfortable for a few days. The cold, the wet and the painful have an appeal for her. I used to say to her maybe it was a middle-class guilt thing and she could get psychiatric help. Joke.

Thanks for the American recipes though I don't know when I'll get the chance to use them. Your horoscope for the month says to take it easy. Bear it in mind. Wear lots of warm things and look after yourself.

Me looking after Marianne. At least it'll make her laugh.

She took me to Switzerland once, skiing. A school trip. Chocolate box lids everywhere. I couldn't believe it. The first thing I did was phone my mother from the top of a mountain shouting I'M CALLING YOU FROM THE TOP OF A MOUNTAIN as if it was significant. I don't know why I thought it made any difference but it's what I did. I can't deny it. The party of kids I was supposed to be looking after were all outside the box yelling so I had to really concentrate to hear anything coming back. It took a while to realise she wasn't saying anything. She was moaning quietly, kind of singing and didn't know who I was. I shouted IT'S ME ME, IT'S ME but it didn't help. She hung up. I fixed my face and went outside looking breezy.

That afternoon the lifts were cancelled because of high

88

winds and drifting. Later, the sound of thunder kept us awake. By morning the snow was thick as porridge and sinking thigh deep. We wore extra clothes and went higher all the time to get out of the fog, the continual blur of more snow, falling like soft boulders. In the end, it was almost impossible to see where we were going. I have weak eyes and no sense of direction anyway so she took the lead: all I had to do was keep her in sight and follow in the same tracks. I didn't even have to cut my own path. I lasted twenty minutes. The snow falling and the cold eating through the layers of cloth just wore me down. It kept coming: bigger than me and not open to reason. I just gave up. The snow could win. I didn't see the point of making a fool of myself competing against something that huge. Marianne got smaller and dimmer, not knowing while I stood in the drifts. Only the faint sound of her skis shushing a path down the mountain away from me. It was possible she'd get to the bottom and never notice. Her tracks were filling already and there was just whiteness, the creaky prickle of flakes on my jacket.

She noticed. A few minutes later, there she was struggling up the faint traces of the path she'd made earlier. I went on standing, skis turned to the hill. Our mouths and noses were covered, eyes obscure behind goggles so we stared at each other's gloves keeping our chins tucked from the bite of flying ice.

What are you doing? she said, a thin little voice in the wind. You can't just wait here.
I looked at a loose piece of stitching on her cuff.
Why not?
I didn't know if she could hear me. I was only speaking to be stubborn.
Why not?
She didn't answer, just stood flexing her hands against the cold to make me feel guilty and stupid. We reached the bottom an hour later. I still don't know what it was I wanted. What I would have done if she hadn't turned, is she hadn't retraced to find me.

I sit on the floor and think about Marianne being the shape ahead in the snow. I don't know what to write. Marianne is 5000 miles away. She lives in a TV full of WALK/DON'T WALK and policemen with guns. The home of the hamburger and hot fudge sundae, the drive-in pizza. The Land of the Brave and the Home of the Free. Blue Grass and Red Necks. It takes a letter six days to reach.

> Do not
> operate machinery
> Avoid alcohol

In bed, I run my hands over the reclaimed ribs, the bony shoulders like wingsprouts. I balance the gin on the edge of the rug and feel the flat bowl of my hips. They're sharp on either side for the first time I remember. Like a man's. Laughter shakes the mattress. I laugh till the neighbours thump the wall.

SOME OF US HAVE WORK TOMORROW.

blood

There is blood on the pillow.

Three brownish miasmas rimmed with pink. Like bacteria on a white dish. I should go to the dentist before this gets worse. My teeth are falling apart.

Something scatters when I reach for the radio, like little rats'
feet making off under the bed. Two red pills wobble on the
side table, left behind in the rush. I slither to the edge of the
bed, rubbing my eyes before I notice it's more than pills over
the floor. A spike of glass just under one dangling foot, more
in corners. Not fragments but big bowl-shaped chunks. It's
not till I go to the bathroom and wash I see the score down
the length of my arm, pink against the fishbelly white. No
blood: just the score, straight and smooth. Another one like
a dotted line tearing between elbow joint and wrist. A neat
row of three jagged pieces glitters on the bathroom ledge. I
can't think what day it is.

Thursday.
The piece of paper beside the cupboard reminds me. I'm
supposed to see Dr Stead today. 9.25. I can't work out how
I slept so long. I pour more coffee and notice my nails are
flaking, white pits chipped into the horn. Dry blood trails
trace the quick. I sit in the kitchen cleaning them with a piece
of blunt glass and drinking more coffee, lots of coffee.

I will not go to work.
I might never go back at all.
This at least is cheering.

DR STEAD 11.30 REMEMBER

I write it several times on the back of an envelope but this
reluctant feeling in my insides gets worse. Something rum-
bling with the stomach acids, making my skin crawl.
Whatever it is doesn't want me to go to the surgery. I watch
it get into my fingers, making them reach for the Vim. I'm
going to leave streaks of cleanser all over the kitchen.

I used to have beautiful hands: white with soft skin. The
wrists so transparent you could see the veins working. In a
good mood, my mother called them Piano Hands. Other
times she called them work-shy. Every second night I

brought out a basket of cosmetic preparations and gave them the once-over, rubbing in cream and filing my nails before the big finish with fresh coats of varnish. Now they chip, sliding on decay in the kitchen. My knuckles go blue in the water. I think about Michael's erection in my hand, the buzz of blood along the shaft. Dirty water oozes under my nails. The cleaning is just a sham. Broken glass crunches on the floor like sugar. I shove unidentifiable debris under the rug and hope it stays put. Superficially everything looks fine but underneath is another story. I never wash out the bin or scour the sink. The grease beneath the cooker turns my stomach but doesn't stop me sweeping more under there: dried up breadcrumbs and frozen peas, flakes of onion skin. The trick is not to look.

I rush through the rest of this performance not knowing what the rush is for. Maybe I really believe the sky is falling. Or the ground might open beneath me and

I'm always preparing for something and never know what it is. I should wash things. The pillowslips haven't been washed for weeks so the patterns of blood stay. There are marks on the sheets too: trails from half-hearted cuts. I don't menstruate but I bleed other ways. The scratches on my wrists purse like clam mouths in the water, refusing to open. I need to pour the water away, get my bag and

something shrill scares hell out of me.

The phone.

The phone ringing. My fault: I wanted it to ring yesterday. Christ. Catching my shoe on the floor-cloth, skidding. I almost break my neck getting there in time then almost don't lift the receiver. I have no consistency.

ME   [Guarded] Hello?
PHONE   Hello there. Listen, I phoned school looking for you
              and they said you were off. So I guessed you'd be
              here, if you see what I mean. [Urbane laugh] Any-
              way, here you are. [Pause for cool effect] It's Tony.

92

	[Pause to let it sink] Listen, how are you fixed for tonight?
ME	[Silence. Can't make sense of the question.]
PHONE	Remember I said I'd take you to the track? She's running tonight, top form. Poetry. And I was thinking who to share the champagne with. Consider this your lucky night. Pick you up about six, take you to the races then maybe a meal. What do you say?
ME	I'm not very well, Tony. [Coughs] I'm really not well.
PHONE	Aw come on. Night out do you good. Fatten you up a bit. That's what you need, amongst other things, and I'll see what I can do about those too. [Throaty chuckle replete with meaning]
ME	No really, I'm not —
PHONE	Look, why don't you come round to the shop since you're off and put in a few hours with me? Always a few extra quid and you can put it on the Queen tonight: guaranteed return. Straight from the horse's mouth eh?
ME	I'm kind of busy this afternoon.
PHONE	What do you mean busy? Look, just an hour or two, that's all. I'll give you a lift back so you can change for tonight if that's what's worrying you.
ME	Well, maybe. I'll think about it OK? But I can't come tonight. [Inspiration] I'm having a meal with Ellen.
PHONE	Break it. She'd understand.
ME	No, I'm sorry Tony. I can't. I really can't. You wouldn't like me to break a promise.
PHONE	Well, worth a try. But she doesn't have all that many runs left this season [Means: There's something wrong with you, going to see an old lady instead of grabbing the chance with me I'm used to better things I can get any amount of girls you know don't you realise what you're being offered here?] Better catch you early next time eh? [Means: I know you're just playing hard to get]
ME	Yes. I'm sorry Tony. I am. I'm sorry.
PHONE	No skin off my nose. I'll forgive you this time. [Means: Don't let it happen again and remember I'm

your boss] Anyhow I have to get back to work. We
don't all have the day off. Ciao.

ME   I'm sorry.

Tony has already hung up. He could be losing business. I
leave the receiver off the hook, cram a few things into a bag
and run leaving the dirty water behind.

By the time the bus comes my hands are frozen and I can feel
blood vessels popping in my cheeks, waiting for ages with
my scarf like a yashmak in case anyone tries to speak to me.
No-one ever does but you can't be too careful. I stay like this
all the way into town to avoid paying the fare, occasionally
pretending to see through the grime on the windows to the
fields beyond, staring to look preoccupied. My heart seizes
every time the conductress turns, clinking money in the
leather bag, spewing tickets from the ratchet. I almost miss
the stop being so purposeful. By the time I reach the surgery
I know I have no intention of keeping the appointment. I
need to keep moving. Thank god I have the notebook.

I'M SORRY I CAN'T COME TODAY. I DON'T WANT TO WASTE YOUR
TIME.
I'M SORRY NOT TO HAVE GIVEN MORE NOTICE. IT WON'T HAPPEN
AGAIN.
I'M SORRY.

Messy. I fold it so the letters don't show and write DR STEAD
on both sides then don't know what to do with the damn
thing. There's no letterbox on the double door.

   It's open.
A woman with a pushchair and a sticky child wait behind
me while I make an obstruction.
   On you go, it's open. You just push.
The child is struggling out of her locked arm, kicking its feet
to find the ground. In a moment it will teeter towards me,
its hands reaching for my coat. I charge at the door with my
head down, plant the note on the desk and leave again
without seeing a thing.

Marianne made the appointment. I had no regular doctor. Right from the first, Dr Stead wanted to handle things his way. The Stead method was drugless: he thought if I took anything it would just delay what he called *full awareness*. It hadn't a chance because the Spanish nurse had jabbed me full of something pretty potent after I took a swing at her. By the time they came to see if I wanted to go to the mortuary I couldn't stand up. I was woozy for almost a week. Dr Stead had been hoping for a more straightforward case. Every time he asked a question I could see he wished he hadn't. But he hung on. Sleeping pills reluctantly, tranquillisers then anti-depressants when the things that were supposed to be passing off didn't. Red ones, yellow ones, green capsules, white tablets that break in half along a screw-top seam. I get more every time I go. He is a proud man and takes it hard. He wanted so much to do it himself. I think about Dr Stead and keep walking further from where he is. Through the precinct, across the lot, between the gap in the railings. The river is in spate and the swans eddy in the current, paddling nearer to the bank. They don't know I have nothing for them to eat. My face runs, thinking about Dr Stead. Poor Dr Stead. I don't tell him the half of what I do. I'm a liar and a cheat with Dr Stead while he sees endless queues of sick people and tries to make room for me. I watch the swans and they watch me, useless at the edge of the water with nothing to give. Eventually they give up interest altogether and drift further downstream.

ooo

Ellen's house is on the slope of a hill, looking out over the town from a distance. From the top of the hill you can see the streetlamps in the town centre, shops locking up for the night, headlamps fogging through the grey like projection beams from the back of the cinema. The street looks like an old movie shot through a vaselined lens but it's not. It's not a film because if you stand in the middle of the road, the traffic swerves to avoid you. You could make holes in the bodywork if you collide. The cold nips through the pockets of my coat because I'm not wearing enough clothes. Change of seasons catching me unprepared. I move one finger after another, counting. Ellen's door is still there.

Ellen had been on holiday herself, to Skye. I was in a downstairs room when she came back. I heard her come in, sound surprised, then Marianne took her into another room to tell her Michael was dead. The voices were very low for a minute so I don't know how she phrased it. Whatever it was, I heard it hit Ellen through two walls and was ashamed. I was invading her house and making her feel terrible. I still do. I can't take that tonight on top of the rest: if she's kind to me I'll only cry and she'll start too. That kind of responsibility makes me desperate. I want someone strong enough to catch me when I fall and that's not Ellen. Yet I keep standing at the door, knowing I won't knock, wondering how much colder it is possible to feel. I don't feel as if I'm really here at all. I'm not really awake. I'm stuck in this half-sleep that won't change. Not today or tomorrow. Because this is the way things are now. This is what is. There is no waking up any more. On the other side of the hill, cars move and shops are closing. I have to put up with this. Time passes in little ways, things alter for no reason.

This is the Way Things Are.
This is What Passes For Now.

I have to put up with Dr Stead and he has to put up with me. I have to take the pills because they will make me accept. They will make me biddable. Maybe they will make me stop wanting to know the answer. Maybe the pills know the answer. I doubt it but I have no proof.

I stand on the slope of hill and look down at the street that is not a film. This is the Way Things Are Now. I touch the wood round the door, the crust of brick. My knuckles scrape on the brick and the skin peels. I look at the blood and try to believe I'm here, that the wood and the brick are the truth. The knowledge of this fact. There is no dream and no waking up. This is today. The Way Things Are.

My knees stiffen and buckle. I know I should move.

Maybe I could go to the beach.
I think about standing on the edge of the cob at the beach, listening to the tide in the dark grey of early winter evening. Rushes touch my legs. The sand looks white. I could lie on this white sand, peel off my clothes and wait. I think about the incoming tide, the waves that never stop.

Romance.

The moon and the stretch of visible sand over the cob. I'm waiting outside Ellen's house, imagining the beach. A little light romantic fiction. Oh well.

I limp like a drunk down the hill with my frozen knees. I have to go home.

ooo

Pale blue paper with ruler lines, folded once across the middle. There's a betting slip behind the door. I pick it up with the tips of my fingers.

TRIED TO PHONE THEN CALLED ON THE OFF CHANCE.
GET YOU AT SEVEN. BE READY. TONY XXX

I try not to think about it as the bath fills.

ooo

Almost pretty.
There I am in the mirror, inoffensive in a dress with a thick belt to show what remains of the curves. New stockings and

97

slingbacks despite the time of year. Lack of practicality is sexy in women's clothes. The gravel and the crouch of brakes outside makes me stare harder. I try not to hear the different size of shoe thudding on the boards.

Hello? Anybody home?
I see Tony from the top of the stairs, holding up a bottle in white paper, green glass and a foil neck pushing up from the tissue like a clumsy orchid.

Anticipation, he says. Always take it for granted I'm going to win.
The lips disappear into his beard and the teeth appear, very white and straight. It's definitely Tony. He tells me I look lovely, a real picture. I want to tell him it's not me but I smile instead. He reaches out his hand and says it again.

You look lovely. You really do.

The car is the wrong colour. It plays Country and Western Music as we ease onto the main road.

She's on form, he says. Should have seen her this afternoon.
The seat creaks with his weight: now we're round the corner, he relaxes.

Called round on the offchance you were home but no such luck. Thought you weren't well? Anyway, she's looking good. Nearly as good as you.
He pats my leg.

Expect a treat tonight.
I know we're talking about a dog and try to think of something appropriate to say. In the pause, he sings along with the tape.

When you're in love with a beautiful woman, it's hard
He looks sidelong to see my reaction, encouraging me to be cute. He keeps doing it between the sentences.

Maybe after the race we could go somewhere. On the town. Assume you haven't eaten. Could do with some more even if you have. Few more pounds and you'd be a stunner. How are things by the way? I always forget to ask. You

98

never look ill to me so I forget to ask.
   Then somebody hangs up when you answer the phone
   Just relax and listen to the music. This one's my favourite.
Dr Hook. Classic. You don't mind if I run it again. You look
great. Should wear a dress more often. Hiding your best
assets.
He looks over again, his face melting on the double-take.
   Christ what did you do to your hands?
I look and see the knuckles bruised and oozy. This is not
feminine.
A dopey voice says Oops. I tripped. Silly me.

I tell myself I am with Tony in his car. I tell myself all the way
to Glasgow.

jesus
jesus
jesus

say it's all right
jesus

blood

There's blood on the pillow.
Glass on the bathroom ledge. A neat row of three jagged
pieces. I step on two stray fragments going back through for

my clothes. I can't think what day it mouth is sticky, my face
bloated because I ate. When I try to brush my hair, strands
fall out, wisping over the sheet. Handfuls coiled up in the
fronds of the brush. Closer to, the eyes are yellow. I put on
two of everything, shivering. Maybe I have a chill.

Almost winter.
I drink black coffee staring out at the missing fence slats.
People outside are going about the day. There's nothing to
see but I keep looking out, convinced there's a detailed
confession running over my forehead, secrets shaping up
in braille goosepimples on my arms. I keep sipping the
coffee.
I couldn't think how to get out inviting him in. Tony
wouldn't give up and go back to the car. He stood for ages.
My stomach was hurting from all the food but I couldn't
think what to say to make him go away. So I let him in. I
admit it, I let him inside the porch. Once he was in here he
pulled me close so suddenly I fell against his chest while he
stroked my hair, the back of my neck.

I said, Won't your wife be wondering where you are?
He didn't say anything. Just smiled, a tight little smile that
made his mouth smaller.

I said, Maybe you better think about going now: it's way
past two. Aren't you tired?

He just did the smile again and pulled me back to lever his
mouth in place. I kissed his ear instead and said I really think
you ought to be going now, don't you? knowing I didn't
have the neck to pretend to pass out if he stayed any longer.
There was every chance I'd keel over, my feet blotted out
with the seep of rain through the open-toed shoes. He held
my chin and made me meet his eyes.

Promise me we can do this again, he said, Promise me.
I think I was smiling, not wanting to but not able to stop.

He said, I've never met anyone like you.

He kissed me again before he went for the car and I came in
and threw up like an animal.
jesus

100

Upstairs, there is blood on the pillow, glass on the

The flap of paper on concrete, receding footfalls. Three pieces of mail lie flat in the porch.
The blue is airmail from America.
The white is from Norma's lawyer.
The manilla is typewritten, giving nothing away.
I leave the others and take the manilla into the kitchen. While the kettle boils, I open it. Slowly.

PSYCHIATRIC comes out first, large print on a buff card.
FORESTHOUSE HOSPITAL WARD1D

The name of a doctor who is not Dr Stead, a phone number and a date. It is today. Dr Stead's referral. I try to read it again while the words fold and slither on the paper.

It is today.

The fat woman rocks in her seat as the hostess recedes. Holding something. A sizzle of bursting polythene.
Broken Romance is it?

She sniffs.
You can tell me. That's something I know all about. I know exactly how it is.

The seat number in front says 13. 13. An air nozzle open as an eye-socket over my head but there is no air. Teeth burst sugar beads near my ear.
You can tell me.

101

My stomach lurches as the carcass tilts and we turn painfully into the stretch of runway. The grass races as the fat woman twists in the seat, her skin almost touching mine. Beneath my feet, the low rumble of the engine rises, reaching my throat.

I remember looking out of the window. There was nothing to see. I remember there being nothing to see.

ooo

You can't miss it, the receptionist said, a single cyclamen pink finger pointing, retracting. You can't miss it.
I missed it and a man in a white dust coat led me back the right way. I handed over the card then brushed something that wasn't there off my lapels while he read it, trying to look casual and collected. Sane.

I ended up in a grey-brown room with matching curtains pulled to keep out the sun. It was too hot in the room but I kept my coat on. By the time the psychiatrist finally turned up, sneaking in as though he didn't want to disturb me, I was poaching. He was wearing a grey and brown suit, tie right up to his neck. What was left of his hair was white and he had liver spots on the backs of his hands, the same colour as the carpet and the curtains. Like camouflage. I wondered if it was deliberate. He kept carefully to the other side of the table, nodding briefly. Once. He started without asking who I was. Maybe it didn't matter.
So, he said. Why do you think you've been sent to us?
He sat, took off his glasses, smiled slowly like a crocodile.

102

I knew right away this was going to be a disappointment.

LESSON 1: Psychiatrists aren't as smart as you'd think.

I knew three things right away:

1. I hate facile questions (So-why-do-you-think-you're-here is so easy to subvert);
2. You have to try: it's the whole purpose of being here; and
3. You have to be on your guard. There is no defence against the arbitrariness of things. You have to be suspicious of everything.

All three things whispered in my ears like Angels and Devils in a TV cartoon which made it very difficult to think straight. Dr One didn't know that. All he knew was I wasn't answering.

So, he said. Why do you think you've been sent to us? He thought I wasn't trying.

LESSON 2: Psychiatrists are not mind-readers. They just try to look as though they are.

He tried another tack.

Tell me from the beginning what you think is making you feel bad, he said. Take your time and tell it in your own words.

For some reason, I hadn't expected this. I'd done that story so many times I knew it like a nursery rhyme but now my throat was contracting. I couldn't think about even the first line without feeling I was about to short-circuit. On top of everything else I was ashamed of how stupid I'd been. I hadn't thought it through. It was perfectly logical he should start like this yet I hadn't seen it coming. The devils whispered *What did you expect? A course of shock therapy the minute you walked in the door?* The angels whispered *Try. Dr Stead went to a lot of trouble to get you this appointment. You have to try.* There was only one way out of this. My mouth knew more than the rest of me put together. I had to trust my mouth. I closed my eyes and the mouth said

103

My mother walked into the sea.

I remember the voice: chiselled as crystal. Cold as a razor.
I hadn't known it would start like this but then I was
redundant. The voice didn't need me. It didn't even like me.
I let the story came out in this disembodied glass voice and
listened, out of harm's way in the corner of the room.

She didn't die right away. At the funeral, the man I lived
with shook my hand. I left him. I had an affair with a
married man. He left his wife to come and stay with me.
Things were difficult. My house started caving in and we
had to move somewhere else. Then we went away and he
drowned

The end of the story seemed to come up too soon. I heard the
last bit twisting out of kilter then stopping without warning.
The room felt suddenly eerie: like the Bates Motel in
Psycho. If you listened hard you could probably hear the
liver-coloured furniture breathing, little creaks and rustles
where people had been before. I had to think hard to
remember where I was.

He drowned.

Something was happening to my stomach. As though I'd
stamped my foot down hard at the end of a staircase and the
floor wasn't where I thought it was. The side of the pool, the
circle of men, blue eyes and the sky. I suddenly remembered
what I was saying wasn't a story. It wasn't the furniture
breathing, it was me. What I was saying was true.

LESSON 3: Psychiatrists give you a lot of rope knowingly.

He waited to let it get worse. It was ages before he said
anything else.

And what are your circumstances now? he said eventually, making it sound like something that had just popped
into his head but I knew he was grinding down my defences
on purpose. I closed my eyes again. It would be easier in the
dark.

I'm starting to hate things. I hate where I work. I see small things about too many small people and it makes me bitter. I don't want to be bitter. Bitterness hurts. I'm lonely. I'm afraid I'll go sour and nobody will love me any more. Something about me kills people. I'm losing days and drinking too much. I'm not a proper woman. I no longer menstruate. Sometimes I think I don't exist. I keep looking for the reasons and never find them, waiting all the time but I don't know what for. I always do the wrong thing.

Cold spots dripped on my upturned palms but I didn't feel it was me crying. I could find no connection between these splashes and me. I connected only with the words. They swelled and filled up the whole room. I was eaten and swallowed inside those words, eaten and invisible. When it was over I knew I was smiling. I had been afraid of wasting his time but now I knew I had performed with dignity. From inside the belly of the words, Dr One looked meagre. He repositioned his specs because he felt uncomfortable and missed one of his ears.

LESSON 4: Psychiatrists are just like all the rest.

There was a bitten triangle of sandwich curled on a blue plate on the ledge behind his desk, pink stuff spilling out the inside. He must have eaten the rest of it. He might even go back and eat this leftover bit later. The idea made me feel sick. He beamed an expanse of bald head in my direction and dazzled me with those yellow teeth. Time for questions about my work. Asinine things: my colleagues and how to organise the day to be under less pressure, my family and how they could be a source of help. My family. This little man with the pink head and dandruff showing through, his tortoise neck rising and falling reaching to my gullet. I clenched my wet fists and glared. What did he think he was here to do for christsake? He knew nothing. He was just a little man being paid to sit here and say the first thing that came into his bald head, rooting for the meaningless nothings that made the life of a complete stranger. It wasn't honest. He didn't understand how little any of this mattered. How little either of us mattered. Contempt gave me a boost. The scored arteries on my wrist throbbed, pulsing with the adrenalin of imminent danger. I felt like an empty tiger. I hoped he knew.

Why are you smiling Miss Stone?
He squinted across the table through those readjusted spectacles.
Why are you smiling?
Didn't he know? He was stuck in this stuffy room in the corner of a psychiatric ward, talking about things of no consequence with an equally absurd stranger, hiding from the sun behind this hideous hemp curtain and he couldn't see it. The sky was passing outside for chrissakes. Planes and birds. People going about their work. The whole thing was insane. I tried a sardonic laugh but it didn't work: bits got stuck on the way out so it sounded more like a cough. I let my head hang back and sighed instead. The rush of blood made me abruptly dizzy. He carried on regardless, saying something in the background but it was just a blur. Tears drained backwards into my ears. I was floating up toward the ceiling, inflating with something like love: serene and distant as the Virgin Mary, radiating Truth from the halo of stars round my head. I knew so much,

There was No Point.
Everything was the Same as Nothing.
And I knew there was nothing he could say.

He knew it too. The room was silent because he had nothing to say any more. Something was uncoiling like a cobra in my throat and sat upright before I choked. The voice was poison.
What do you suggest I do to make it all better doctor? He drowned for christsake. He *drowned*.

He looked back blankly. I was going to have to spell it out.

There's no fucking point, is there?

106

Mistake. This time it came out petulant. I knew he was getting me side-tracked, undermining my certainty. He smiled like a crocodile and clicked the top of his pen.

How do you know things will never be different? Isn't it all a matter of time? You are obviously an intelligent human being. An intelligent woman. Surely your rational mind tells you this bad time will fade? No?

You're missing the whole point, I said flatly, staring hard at the wall.

So what do you think the point is? he said, ingenuous as hell.

I breathed deep and remembered my training. I was a teacher after all. I could cope with goading.

What you have just described is the whole point. The whole point is that time passes. That things fade. He is already hard to remember. Look, I used to cry because I thought I'd forget. Then I knew that was ridiculous and cried because I remembered. But the truth is that one is the same as the other. Remembering and forgetting are the same bloody thing. He is not alive any more. That's all there is to know. There is no purpose to any of it. The point is there is no point.
The point is
The point is
The point

There was only the sound of blood in my ears and the doctor being quiet on purpose. I was tired to the bone.

LESSON 5: Psychiatrists set things up the way they want them.

Maybe you better come in anyway, he said reasonably. Even if you don't see the point.
I said nothing.

Just for a little while, he went on. For my own good. I was a danger to myself like this. I should come in for a short stay. Just a few weeks. He wondered why I didn't say anything. My bed could be available from Monday. Just a few weeks.

107

Persistence gets me every time. I haven't got any.

A few weeks? I said, not much louder than a whisper. I started crying again. The power had shifted completely to the other side of the desk without my noticing how he did it.

A few weeks, he said. He was very definite.

I had never imagined weeks. I looked at the plate with the piece of sandwich, pink tongue lolling out under the buttery slats of white bread. They would find out I didn't eat.

Two weeks anyway.

I thought about Dr Stead and how much I wanted to feel less terrible and how hopeless it was.

What do you say?

I thought it would only be a few days. What about my work?

An unsubtle digression: right-minded citizen worrying about her contribution to society. Even Dr One would see through that. I couldn't say what was really worried me. What really worried me was the idea of supervision, mealtimes, other people. And the terrible knowledge it wouldn't make any difference anyway. I said none of that. After a long silence, he took a big crumpled hanky out of his drawer and flicked it across. I picked it up and blew my nose, whispering through the crushed cotton.

I don't know, doctor. I don't know.

Like Little Girl Lost. I make myself sick.

Dr One looked at the runny nose and red eyes. He didn't know me from Eve.

I think you should come in for at least two weeks. That's my recommendation. Think about it then ring this number. The bed won't wait past Monday so don't think about it too long. It's up to you what you decide.

LESSON 6: Psychiatrists are devious and persistent. They always win in the end.

I took the piece of paper and left with my head up, up like Jean Brodie. But I knew I'd phone sooner or later. I knew I'd be back on Monday.

108

ooo

Next afternoon, I took the bus for miles.
The streets were frantic. The first shop I went into was just
to get out the way. All it did was take me into another crowd,
hauling at an octopus of sweaters in a sale bin near the door.
Back outside, I couldn't think straight and tried to cross the
road before I should have. A car drove up too fast and too
close. I could feel the heat off the engine through the jacket.
The driver thought it was my fault. He sounded his horn so
loud I thought I would faint on the tarmac. Except I never
faint. He had to slew to the side to get by. Two more cars
hooted before I was clear. It started to rain. The pavement
was seething by this time, damp coats not looking where
they were going, puncturing any space with umbrella spikes.
Then I saw the red cubicle across the street. People parting
like the Red Sea round the safe, glass walls. I pushed towards
that callbox like a swimmer for the far shore. Light and free.
I was going to hospital to be made better. Somebody else's
problem.

ooo

Marianne calls to ask how I am.
I tell her about hospital and she says I've made the right
decision. She says How do you feel? and I tell her I'm
nervous but I know I'm making the right choice. Nobody
needs to worry about me.

On Saturday I tell Allan and he tells me I'm making the right
decision. Tony says nothing all afternoon: big race.
I go to see Ellen with my nicotine hair and tell her about Dr
One. She shows me wool and tells me I'm making the right
decision.

On Sunday David phones to ask how I am. I tell him I'm making the right decision, nobody needs to worry about me.

He says, I won't manage this weekend. Maybe Monday.

I think and say I won't be here on Monday.

No, he says. Right enough. Where will you be? What ward I mean?

I don't know.

Pause. Will you be in the following weekend?

I don't know.

He sighs and says, Well when are visiting times? and I say I don't know. I don't know anything.

I'll get in touch somehow, he says. Good Luck.

I keep the phone at my ear, listening to the line.

Upstairs it takes an hour to find the holdall. The holdall still smells of suntan lotion and grass. His boots topple beneath the empty cloth limbs on the rail.

ooo

Four roads converge from the surrounding fields to the carpark. The carpark is at the foot of the hills. Foresthouse Hospital sits at the top of the hills, a shoebox slatted through with glass. You can't miss it.

I thought Dr One would be there. It was someone else: nothing like Dr One. He asked my name and went out. Hospitals are busy and under-resourced. I know that and try to be patient.

Someone else comes and settles into Dr. One's chair. He says

So. Why do you think you've been sent to us?

someti
that fe
deja vu

I say Sorry? and he says

So. Why do you think you've been sent to us?

110

I blink once and say, Dr One told me to come in. I'm here
by invitation.
Yes, but why do you think you were referred? What's the
problem *as such?*
I stay deliberately calm and collected.
Look, I did all this. I told all this to Dr One just three days
ago. I did all this for Dr One. Maybe there are some notes.
This is a bid to sound polite and helpful. The man looks up.
That may be so but this is different. This is for records.
For *records.*
But I did all this. I'm sure there must be notes. I've been
through all this already. I was told to come here. You must
have it on record already for heavensake.
The man looks as though he just sucked a lemon unexpect-
edly.
I'm just here to make a few notes. Relax. Take your time.
There's no need to get upset.

This is clever. I didn't think I was upset. I was anxious but
I didn't think I was upset. Nonetheless I have to prove it. He
looks young. He looks nineteen. I think about David being
nineteen and tell myself not to be patronising. I take a deep
breath. I tell him the story.

He makes notes and sniffs compulsively, crossing and
uncrossing his legs. I hit on the notion that this could be
some sort of test to see if I've been lying and consciously try
to make the story sound the same as before. He says nothing
when it's finished and doesn't close the door on the way out.

There's a tear in the curtain since last time. Or maybe I just
didn't see it.
Didn't know what you took. Black all right?
A different man comes in, holds out a white plastic cup. It's
hot enough to melt fingerprints.
Coffee, he says. Better bet than the tea.

111

I sit the cup on the floor before I drop it and wait while the new man attempts to settle into the previous man's chair. He's about a foot taller, so this isn't easy. He bangs his shin and pretends it was nothing just the way I'm pretending not to feel the burns on my fingers. We want to be businesslike.

He says, So. Why do you think you've been sent to us?

sometim
this feeli
deja vu

Sorry?

He gets as far as

So. Why do you think...

before I snap.

Look, I say, Why are you asking me this? half an octave too high and too loud. I want to shout Someone else just did that. Just minutes ago, the same thing. This is the third time I've been asked this same old stuff. Doesn't anybody keep any notes around here? Why do you all ask the same thing? But I don't. I cough and try to look reasonable, mustering a reasonable voice.

A doctor just left. He asked me all that.

My foot tips the cup and it slops a little, scalding through my sock. The man grins. Crumbs dance in his moustache. There has been a *misunderstanding*. The man who just left isn't a doctor. He is a *nurse*. Just taking notes of my details. But now the doctor is indeed here. He is Dr Two.

Hello, he says. Hello.

I ignore the outstretched hand and ask if I can see Dr One. Dr One has my details already. Couldn't I see Dr One?

Dr Two says AHHHH. AHHHHHHHHHH.

This means what comes next is something I'm not going to like. He is very sorry. Dr One isn't here often. Comes in to help out every so often. Really retired. But I can have every confidence in Dr Two. I can relax. I can take my time. There's no need to get upset.

sometim

Maybe this is a technique: something clever to do with familiarity and contempt or feeling worse before you feel

112

better. I wonder about this as the story makes rounds of my mouth like a rat in a wheel. Maybe this is therapy.

Maybe

ooo

A bed on the left hand side of the double row of four is full of sleeping fat lady. The rest are empty. The uniform-free MOIRA leads me to the full one. We stop and look down on the fat lady. MOIRA's name-badge droops when she frowns.
Betty shouldn't be here. This is yours. Betty here again. They keep putting her here.
She lifts one of Betty's eyelids then leaves me alone with the unconscious carcass. I fish out a crossword puzzle book and sit on the chair next to the locker, filling any word that fits into the right number of boxes without reading the clues. Two men come and put Betty on a trolley while I pretend not to look. They change the top sheet and MOIRA comes back. None of them have any uniforms. She sellotapes my name to the locker door and tells me to get into bed now. I say I'm perfectly fit and she smiles. It is nothing to get upset about. Just routine. All new patients spend the morning in bed. They get up in the afternoon. I can get up in the afternoon. Then I'll fit in just fine, just fine.

Pink pyjamas (girls' age 11)
Change of clothes
Pencil sharpener
Photos
Books and notebook

My name in someone else's writing shows through the selloptape on the side of the locker. They bring screens to let you change.

113

What will I do while I'm lasting Marianne? What will I do?

12.00: The doctor gives me three red pills and a cup of water, sounds chest and looks in mouth. Staff nurse tells him my name. He picks up the crossword book and raises an eyebrow. I fill in menu card and accept receipt of a pamphlet of regulations and visiting times. He says maybe I'd like to sleep now. The nurse brings a cup of tea. Sugared. I don't drink it.

1.00: A different nurse (in uniform) comes past the curtain.

    Oh. Dr. Wilson?

She doesn't even notice I'm there. I wait till she turns and look hostile. She doesn't notice again.

    No sign of Dr. Wilson. He's on rounds?

I say, No, no sign of Dr. Wilson.

She says, Had lunch Yes?

I say, Had lunch Yes.

She doesn't look back as she leaves.

1.30: A man comes with a plate. Stew and chips. I say I had lunch first sitting. I already had lunch. Besides, I'm vegetarian. He looks at the cup of cold tea and back at me. But he takes the plate away.

2.00: ʙᴇɴ brings me three red pills and another glass of water. He says Hello there by way of introduction then I swallow. I get more sweet tea as a reward.

3.00:

Dear Marianne,

I'm bored out of my mind (joke) and only been here one day. The ward is a rectangular space with beds at equal distances. The beds are grey metal frames with matching equidistant lockers. The lockers have an upper box which is open and a lower with a door. They don't lock. There are names sellotaped to the lockers with clear tape. The card beneath the tape is yellow with blue biro letters in block capitals. My bed is one from the door open end of the ward and two from the window end. The window has crimson curtains: the entrance to the ward is open. The floor tiles are white, green and blue. Behind my locker there is a toilet and shower block. The covers on the beds are crimson and the sheets white. There are two pillows for each bed, eight beds in the ward. The beds are single and cranked very high. There is no-one else but me.

At four o'clock someone comes to take the screen away. I ask if I can get up yet and she doesn't even look in my direction to check.

Of course, she says. No-one's stopping you.
The screen squeals and clanks like rusty chains all the way down the corridor.

I sit up. Nothing. I sneak out of bed, dress in the same clothes I took off earlier then sit on the covers. I make the bed then sit on it again. Second time I stand up, I notice the tiles are a little blurry. And I'm thirsty. Not enough to drink the sugary tea but thirsty. I think about washing my hair in the shower with my head tilted back for the water. But maybe they don't let you take a shower whenever you like. The regulations say nothing you want to know. They don't say where to get a drink or when you can have a shower. My knees fold oddly when I walk.

I find my sea legs in the green and bue corridor. A man at the glass partition of the reception bay is filing little bits of buff card. I ask if it's OK to go for a walk. He doesn't look up, just keeps shuffling cards.

Of course you can. Of course, of course.

I walk away slow to give him the time to change his mind. People do.

Just round the grounds.
I shout walking backwards to keep an eye on his face, fishing for the remaining armhole of my black coat. Maybe he doesn't know I'm a patient.

I won't go anywhere, just round the grounds.

Sure, he says. Remember back for tea, still filing. Party. Just around the grounds.

My voice has a little echo. He keeps his eyes on the cards and his face fuzzes over. I get woozier with every step.

It's freezing.
No moon and cloud over the stars. I stop and wait for my pupils to enlarge, finding enough light to keep me on the straight and narrow round the white hospital block. It's soft underfoot and the boots make no noise. Moss. It cracks its way through the paving and makes me stumble. But I keep going. The path stops abruptly behind the maintenance block. Off the track the ground is marshy. There is a slow suck on the soles and worms of fluid between my toes. One-legged, I stumble, bump into a wall in the dark: a low, flat building with no windows. The sign is blurry and I have to hold it down to read. It takes a moment or two to come clear. MORTUARY. Just like the thing. I go for a walk and find the dead centre of town. White breath scatters from my mouth and nose when I laugh and the skin on my teeth frosts over. I lean back against the sign, wondering how long I can last out here. Maybe I could wait till the meals are over. Only the cold keeps me awake and cunning.

I didn't go and see my mother in the mortuary. I didn't want her laughing at me, falling for a trick. Besides, the under-taker warned us she had hit herself against the fire-tiles. The living room had been full of the sweet smell of turned ham. I know it doesn't make sense now but I didn't go. I was sorry afterwards but there's no going back on it. I didn't go.

In Spain, they had to talk me out of the room where they kept Michael after I got dopey from the injection. I felt like my skin was on fire. They told the courier to take me for a walk and he left it to his girlfriend. She took me for miles. Maybe it wasn't far at all but it seemed that way. When I started to buckle she called a taxi. She put me to bed in their flat and told me to sleep. I swallowed the whole bottle of tranquillisers I'd been taking at home and half a bottle of their vodka. The only thing I could find to write on was a magazine. I wrote YOU'VE BEEN VERY KIND. THANKS across Joan Collins' face on the cover. Then I lay back down again.

116

I felt too shaky to sleep but I tried. The vodka was a mistake. After ten minutes or so I threw up into their en suite sink, right down to the bile. When the courier's girlfriend came to fetch me for the mortuary I was out cold. It took her all morning just to get me to stand up. By the afternoon they had started the post-mortem so I missed that one too.

MORTUARY.

I've never been this close to one before. The sign comes and goes. My vision doubles. I have to feel my way in the wavering dark, the soles of my boots seeping through the moss.

ooo

You need to lift it higher. Higher. It'll just unravel.
There are three women in the ward. Two are wrapping bandages round each other's arms. The other one issuing orders has a devil mask and a nurse's uniform. It's the first I've seen today. They turn and look as I walk, the loosening sole of my boot scraping on the tile.
We're mummies, one says, smiling behind the bandage. Mummies.
The devil mask says I am almost late for the party. The uniform isn't just a costume.
I tell the nurse maybe I should go to bed. I don't feel so good.
But it's for everybody, she says. Everybody.
The women behind her hold their mouths open like baby birds while she splashes red liquid onto their teeth, hollows out their eyes with black make-up.
Aren't you dressing up?
They let me come in my coat and boots.
The dining room is low-lit, orange from crepe lanterns. I hadn't anticipated so many men. The nurses encourage them to dance. There is blurry accordion music and nurses twirling underwater in the arms of these men. One hand has

117

blue tatooed crosses on the knuckles. My ears swim to the Gay Gordons. It's too hot. In the corner, an old woman in a wheelchair picks green icing off a piece of cake. Under a pointy hat with a crepe frill, another is crumbling biscuit between her fingers, muttering like a rosary gone wrong. One of the dancing men shouts hooch. MOIRA wobbles toward the table with a white plate, a potato and beans, a glass of emerald fizz.

Enjoy yourself, she says, rippling as she walks away.

My eyes water. The heat off the plate is making me dizzy. The potato skin is baked crisp and flecked with salt like a shore pebble, oozing with the red spawn of beans. The green lemonade hisses. I notice just before the table comes up to smack my cheekbone. I wait with my face on the tablecover while the music gets louder. Hooch. A cowboy and a white-coated nurse appear at the ends of the hands that haul me straight then we go together, my feet unsteady and my arms stretched like a crucifix, trawling across the dancefloor to the corridor, the luminous ward with creaky beds too high off the ground. My hair drips sauce. I don't know where to put my clothes, how to fold them.

It took three weeks to get him home. They had to call every day to check. Not to me, though. He had been reappropriated. He was not my business. He would come back to other people. His wife phoned to say I couldn't see him before the funeral. In the end the casket was sealed so there was no argument. But it was an interesting tactic.

I didn't eat.
I ordered a heart-shaped wreath covered in red car-

nations. Things would be better once the funeral was over.

The call to let me know I could go to the funeral was interesting. It shocked me. The pretence that my presence or absence were someone else's to decide. It was also a reminder they might make life difficult if I didn't play along. A lot of things had never occurred.

I waited all the time to see what was permissible. If I was permissible.

I'm shaky but I know I'll sleep. I've been this way before.

ooo

You can see the corridor striplight from here. It's on all the time, all day and all night. They could put it off for all I know when we're unconscious but I don't think so. I think it's on all the time.

Dear Marianne,
I'm bored out of my mind (joke) and only been here one day.

This isn't true any more but what the hell. She'll make adjustments. The letter is in the back of my notebook. The front is full of other notes: big letters to make it easy to read at a distance. The double vision wears off by the afternoon, but I sometimes forget things. I get over-excited and forget things. I keep the notepad with me all the time, in case.

119

Excuse the script. I'm writing on my knees, in the
visitors'waiting area because there aren't any visitors in it. Everything is pale blue or turquoise or
white. Colour therapy. Colours of the sea. I have
my knitting and four needles under the chair.
Nobody fleeced me for anything sharp yet. There
is a lot of waiting. No point in trying to rush
things one of the nurses said: everything in its
own good time. Its natural to me to learn fast.
Everything in it's own good time means slowly.

I know I should post it before it gets heavier and expensive.
I'm just not ready yet.

Please find enclosed one set of regulations so you
can visit. HAH. Visiting is open everywhere in the
hospital except here. This is because we need our
rest. There aren't many written rules. Most of
them work on the landmine principle: they just let
you loose till you trip on them. I'm not supposed
to lie in or on bed or stay in the ward during the
day. I have to get permission to go outside in case
someone is looking for me. There is a dining
room where we have to eat together, a laundry
room and a waiting area. I am allowed to sit here
and in the dayroom but the dayroom is full of
smoke and makes my eyes water. Everybody
smokes. Maybe I'll get lung cancer ha ha.
I've been for two walks round the grounds. There
is nothing to see. Nothing else has happened.

The lift opens suddenly and makes me jump. Every time I
hear something I swivel and the plastic seat squeals like a
stuck pig. This time it's the WVS trolley. 10.30 They never
have anything I want.

Things could be worse. I haven't seen a doctor
yet: only pills at the moment. I can't see straight.
I'm being good. I fill in my menu cards, take

120

medication when I'm told, say please and thank you. You wouldn't recognise me.

I score out the last bit and put *you'd be proud of me* instead.

Janey comes over and asks for a match. She knows from asking twice this morning already I don't have matches but she asks anyway. People steal her matches. She doesn't believe I have none. She sits beside me pulling her ear-ring so the pierced hole in her lobe stretches out of shape. I flip the letter out of sight and my notes appear.

WHEN DOES TREATMENT START
HOW DO I MAKE APPOINTMENTS
WHAT DO I DO MEANTIME
WHAT ARE THE PILLS FOR

They're of no interest. Janey crosses the carpet to play with the lift buttons. Janey has been here longer than anybody else. She knows things but won't give anyone else any clues. Maybe she needs to keep her system secret to be able to work it. The lift comes with nothing in it. Janey's slippers scuffle into the distance as someone's heels clop closer. Norah arrives hugging her own shoulders just as the lift disappears. She asks for a match.

Disny matter. Just thought I'd ask. Off chance.

When the lift won't come she bangs the call buttons hard.

I pick up the pen, flip the notebook and write.

I'm trying, Marianne. I do want to know how to get better. I wait to see doctors but there is nothing fixed. Maybe this is part of the therapy. I don't know. Ros says she has seen a psychiatrist twice. She has been here a long time. I know I have to try.

Norah kicks the wall and presses all the buttons on the lift till they jam.

121

ooo

When you ask if it's OK to go shopping they say yes of course. Of course.

Supermarkets were where Paul and me used to play at grownups. Every Saturday morning he would come to get me from my mother's house in his beat up first car and we would drive to the supermarket. We would patrol the shelves with a trolley and buy maybe four or five things, usually sweeties. But it was something to do together. Teenagers. Today I give the supermarket a wide berth and slip down the alley past the church billboard.
     GOD IS THE MISSING INGREDIENT IN THE CAKE OF LIFE

It's nearly November and Woolworth's is full of garden furniture. People are looking at it as well. I skirt the umbrellas and head for the record counter. You can spend hours there, browsing. Lots of C&W, disco and harmless pop. Michael had lots of records we never got round to playing what with one thing and another. I sorted through it myself too late. The one that really took me by surprise was the Perry Como album. Perry Como. I couldn't figure it out at all. One of the girls in red check dances behind the counter to something I never heard before. The third time it plays, I check my watch and head back to the bus stop. Shopping over. I have a meeting to attend.

The Ward Meeting
The middle of the room is taken up with two rows of old ladies, orderly as potato drills, looking up at a TV that isn't on. My group are at the far side with a man. The man wears

122

a lapel badge with TOM in red letters. TOM is in charge.
Naturally. I sit next to Ros.

Eventually, TOM sighs.
   Well, we can't wait any longer. I think we'll just start.
He nods at everyone and checks our names. Ros is here.
Janey is here. Norah is here. Kathy isn't. I'm not on the list.
   Oh. Teacher.
His eyes flatten out.
   We get quite a few of your lot in here.
I smile in case it's a joke, keeping my head down in case it
isn't. You can't be too careful.
WARD MEETING 1D. Big letters at the top of his clipboard.
TOM leans forward confidently.
   Right. Ah...
He scratches a shaving cut on his neck and looks back to the
big letters to renew his sense of purpose.
   Right. Now the first thing is something I'd rather we
didn't have to discuss. But we have to talk about it just the
same. Pause.
   Fruit. I'm sure you all know what I'm talking about when
I say fruit.

Ros looks at the ceiling and coughs. Norah's cigarette
glows.
   Some of Janey's fruit has gone missing from her locker.
Two apples and um...something.
   A kiwi fruit. Two apples and a kiwi fruit.
Janey gets in before he finds the words on his sheet.
Her arms cross her chest tight enough to restrict respiration.
The voice is wheezy too.
   Two apples and a kiwi fruit, right. Just checking haha.
Anyway, they've gone missing. Now does anybody have
anything to say?

Somebody shouts CHEAT and cards riffle. Norah breaks first.
   You're saying somebody stole it.
Janey flexes. Ros keeps looking at the ceiling.
   No, she says. I think what he's meaning is it could have
been left lying or something. Maybe somebody from the

other wards took it by mistake.

Norah is in no mood.

Oh aye. And I don't think.

Half her cigarette frazzles away and threatens to melt her lipstick.

It wasny me anyway. Bloody kiwi bloody fruit.

Nobody said it was. Nobody said that.

Ros pushes the fringe out of her swollen eyes.

I'm just asking if you have any ideas about it. Getting to the truth here, says TOM. Nobody's saying it was one of you. Us.

Janey snorts and crosses her legs, opens her mouth and closes it again.

So. Have we any more ideas?

Ros keeps trying hard. She tries two unlikely explanations. Norah cuts through the third.

Wouldny put it past some of them just to lift it. Leave things lying. There's all sorts in and out these wards. All bloody sorts. Anyway folk that leave things lying deserve all they get.

She pounds the fag butt to confetti in the ashtray.

Right. Is that us? Nobody has any. OK. Well. Maybe we should move on.

A song quivers over our heads from the line of armchairs, thin as thread. St Theresa of the Roses. Janey sniffs. The sniffs develop a regular pulse. TOM moves on.

Right. OK. I've brought the paper for us to have a look at. See? We could do a bit of topic work here.

He holds up the front page of the Glasgow Herald and points to a headline about jobless totals. Young People in Crisis. He reads out a bit of the article in a loud voice and looks round.

Who would like to say something about this?

Norah lights a fresh fag and flails her arm like a machete.

Ros says, Well, I think it's a bad thing. It's terrible. Nobody wants to see that sort of thing. What else can you say?

TOM doesn't know either. He wants us to know. He nods at Norah.

What, she says.

What do you mean what? I'm asking what you have to say about this article. The Young People in Crisis here? What do you think?

What do you mean what do I think about it? What do you think I bloody think?

I don't know. That's why I asked you.

Christ.

She jerks forward so suddenly, TOM ducks.

Young People my arse. Get a job if they bloody-well looked. Bloody tellies and videos and money for to make theirselves junkies don't tell me about Young People in bloody Crisis.

Janey's head hangs over her chest and she starts to cry. Nobody does anything: there's always somebody crying in the dayroom. You get used to it. TOM gets steely.

Well. What about you, then? Teacher? What do you think? Tell me what you think. Must have an opinion. Never met a teacher without an opinion.

Somebody shouts SNAP.

ooo

The window is huge. It wraps the ward like a cinema screen. From two floors up you look out to fields full of reaped remains and turned earth, a spread of slate sky. Smoke from the factory four miles south. The hummocks in the grounds are meant to slow the cars down. The earth shows through. Hospital signs: white with black letters and arrows. There is no sign to 1D. Not from the front anyway. The road cuts between the field and the hospital like a graphite pencil line. The bus stop at the entrance has a red cross to show the stop, like a teachers' mark in a jotter. Wrong.

Nassim tells me to shoo.

On you go. Nothing to see out there. You think too much

125

always looking out of the window. Bad for you. You should go into the dayroom see a film. Maybe they have a video. Shoo.

ooo

The doctor is over an hour late. An entirely different man to Dr Two. But questions involve risk and I don't want to look picky. I follow him down the sea-coloured corridor to a room with no pictures and all the curtains closed. It smells like dog in the rain. Dr Three doesn't waste any time.

DR THREE [Sitting] Well?

Leather elbow patches on his horrible jacket glint in the gloom. Behind the specs his eyes are all iris.

PATIENT   [Mesmerised] Well what? I thought you would start.
DR THREE   Start what? Start what? You asked to see me. You are the one who knows what this is about.
PATIENT   I've been here nearly a week.
DR THREE   Yes. So what can I do for you?
PATIENT   [Confused. Has forgotten and is trying to remember.] Treatment. I want to know about treatment.
DR THREE   [Leans back with an ominous creak] I don't know what sort of thing you expected. There's no set procedure for these things. You ask to see one of us when you feel you need to. So. Any other questions?
PATIENT   I have to think. [Silence]
DR THREE   Well?
PATIENT   [Nothing. Eyes filling up.]
DR THREE   [Draw a long breath through the nose, leaning back on the chair] How long have you been here did you say?
PATIENT   Nearly a week. I haven't seen anyone.

126

DR THREE   [Sighing] I suppose you want a pass. [Silence] To
           go home for the weekend? You should be going
           home on pass. Getting out of here and facing up
           to things on the outside. You can go out on pass
           any time you like, all right?
PATIENT   No. I don't understand any of this.
DR THREE   I don't know what that's supposed to mean.
PATIENT   It's too fast. You're rushing me.
DR THREE   All right. Take your time. [Silence] Right then.
           Good day.

He taps the bundle of papers on his desk, then folds his arms.
The interview is finished. PATIENT stands thinking maybe
this is some kind of therapy.

DR THREE   The interview is over. [Opens a drawer. The stack
           of papers flake dangerously. He pretends not to
           notice.]

ooo

Cooee. Anybody home?

Bet it was Dr Three. It was Dr Three wasn't it?
Ros blames herself. She knew she should have said some-
thing this morning and didn't. He gets these headaches.
Migraine or something. Apart from that he's a total pig.
She blames herself.

ooo

Nassim tells me to shoo.
I find an empty room at the end of the corridor. A table and
chair.

127

I look at what I've written. A week's effort.
I write TOMORROW

After another while I write WORK.
I rehearse what I will say to the men, to Mr Poppy and Allan and Tony. I have been here one week. I thought I would be on the road to recovery/ the right lines/ the way home. Maybe Nassim is right: I think too much. Thinking is no way to behave in here. I wait for the medicine trolley, willing it to appear.

ooo

Ha Ha Ha Ha Ha.
Tom guffaws all the way down the corridor.
I thought a pass would be something tangible. Like a railway ticket or an identity card or something. All it meant was I could leave after eleven. Transactions with the pharmacy are conducted by phone in case you lose (ie forget) details and get the wrong (ie more) drugs. Everything is done down the wire. Patients need have no knowledge of the details of their pass at all. Not so much as a bit of paper. Tom is hysterical because I don't know. When I leave with my holdall two hours later, he waves and laughs all over again.

Two bills and News of a Mystery Gift get crushed when I open the door. It's musty in the porch, hollow with an unfamiliar smell. I find myself opening the inner door softly, scanning. It's just because I haven't been it smells of someone else. But I'm conscious of my hands being small, the breadth of my back as an easy target. I crash through to the kitchen refusing to look upstairs. It has to be all right.
A couple of days after I started back at work, just say two

128

months ago, the house was broken into. I'd been out somewhere I can't remember and didn't even notice to begin with, just made tea and watched TV in the living room. Poltergeist. I thought the hair bristling on my neck was just from the house settling and from watching the movie: horror pictures affect me that way. Then something thudded and rolled upstairs. A draught made the curtains pouch. I turned off the TV and put on every light I could from downstairs and went up one step at a time.

I knew the worst at the top of the landing. The bedroom door was off the catch. Inside, it was like another room altogether: the quilt on the floor, sheets turned, drawers emptied out. Cheap ear-rings and underwear all over the boards. Some of the clothes had been hauled off the rail and dumped. Michael's coat was still sitting there like the headless coachman, hunched up against the open window. The first thing I thought after it clicked was how little he'd gotten away with. All that trouble and nothing worth his while. I called the cops from the end of the road and asked for Graham. He wasn't on duty but they sent somebody else. A battery, in fact. I reassured them everything was OK, they didn't need to worry about me. After the excitement with the houseful of CID rattling the windows I found the lacquer jewellery box under the bed. It was empty. They'd taken my mother's wedding ring, my engagement ring and a brooch from Michael. A cheap one but still. Nothing else. Downstairs looked fine. I just hadn't known anyone had been there at all. Every so often it feels as though it's happened again but I'm always wrong. So far. I check, make tea and wait. Allan won't be long.

  Big money on the two o'clock.
Tony develops an American soap accent when he's under pressure so we know to work quietly while he plays Mr Big. Allan nods at Tony to make me look. Tony is chewing his moustache. He has a pen mark on his nose and doesn't know. Unexpected bonus. Mr Poppy keeps on his side of the wire.

Hello, Stranger.

Ellen is all concern. I tell her Foresthouse is OK. Really.

Hospitals aren't very nice at the best of times, she says. Douglas wanted out of hospital as soon as it was obvious. Douglas was Mr Holmes. Her eyes fill up. I make her promise not to visit. Next, she has a surprise. I follow her through to the kitchen, feeling uneasy in case it's a cake. She stops at the side of the freezer and smiles, opening the door.

Look.

She shuffles some reddish bundles behind a pale blue haar of ice. It is full of lumps of meat, the blood frozen solid in the muscle so it doesn't leak.

A whole lamb, she says. Just look at it all.

On the way home I check the capsules in my pocket. 10. 10 sugar pills to last a day and a half. I take the night dosage walking home. Maybe exercise will make it work quicker.

Sunday is coming.

This time tomorrow I'll be back in Foresthouse. I don't want to be there either. I walk across the moorland between the town and the Boot Hill towers listening for noises in the dark. All sorts of lunatics hang around the estate waiting for what turns up. I used to walk with a knife in my pocket but stopped after a while. I wouldn't be able to use it if I had to. Also I might be arrested for carrying an offensive weapon. I keep walking up the middle of the road, following advice from a magazine about how not to get raped. Not too fast and not too slow. Looking as though you're in control. Sunday is coming. Que sera etc. There is no telling what the next minute brings.

Ros saw his picture on the locker and asked me who he was.

That's David, I said. David.

Is he family or what? She said the last bit all strung out, wanting the *or what* to be interesting.

It's just David, I said. His name's David.

I didn't know what else to say.

David was someone in Sam's class. I thought he was moody and unpredictable. Our paths crossed a lot at school though I never taught him. He sat next to me in the dinner hall now and again. We may even have waltzed at a school dance. I forget. We liked each other for no particular reason. The unpredictable was attracive then. Anyway, he turned up in my classroom two days after my mother's funeral, returning a supply of books because he was leaving. We did the *so what are you doing now* number for a while then he asked me how I was. He looked shy when I didn't get it. He wanted me to talk about my mother. We went for a drink. He drove me home and we talked in the car. It was me who started it. I kissed his neck. Out of the blue. I started to undress him in the car. Paul was on some management course for work: I never knew what the hell they were about but they took him away overnight. Often. I asked David if he wanted to stay over. Very grown-up and casual. I tried not to overhear the call to his mother, the excuse about staying with a friend. Maybe I was pretending hc was Paul. I don't think so but it's impossible to be sure. The day after my mother's funeral. Christ.

He visited or rang occasionally when I moved to the cottage, sometimes stayed. College was good and he always had plenty to say. After a while he had plenty to do and didn't come at all. I had plenty to do too. He sent a card at Christmas, a present. I called but he was never in.

Six days after Michael's funeral, he turned up at Ellen's door. I knew he had come into the room without looking up because the air turned thick. I didn't know what to expect from him. I never did. He was very cautious and his hair was bleached, just back from holday. Marianne made tea and we were very civilized. Later, I overheard them talking in the kitchen, washing dishes.

So how is she? he said.

Pretty good. Better.

The dishes clattered for a minute before David spoke again.

This is *good?*

Marianne sighed. I turned to leave and the last bit came over my shoulder. David's voice.

She shouldn't get dependent on any one person again.
Not on one person.
I didn't know what he meant.

A couple of days later, we went out, Marianne and me, the
two boys, driving in the car. It became a habit. Marianne
went to America and Sam to University so David kept up the
visits on his own. At first we went out just the same as if the
others were there then gave up the pretence. We stayed in
and drank instead. I drank more than him. There was an
undertone of sex to all this but only by association: depression isn't sexy. But I wanted to be touched. I wanted very
much to be touched. It made me wonder if it would be better
not to see him any more. I said as much once and he just
laughed. I didn't pursue it.

Then he turned up at the house unexpectedly. Wednesday;
not when he would usually call. It was late and he'd been
drinking. I was inside a blanket at the foot of the stairwell,
hair wet and spikey from the bath. The floor was covered in
cut cloth. I had to get up to put a record on to kill the silence.
I didn't know how to talk to him without being drunk. He'd
been swimming, he said. You could smell the chlorine
through the beer. The beer was pretty strong. He pulled me
beside him on the threadbare carpet and said to lie still and
listen. I lay still listening.

sometim

Heartbeat and salt male smells through the warm shirt.

The stubs of hair on the backs of his fingers looked magni-
fied as though some kind of film was peeling off my eyes.
The white rubbed grain of denim on his jeans looked deep
as a duvet. There was a stain on the rug near his heel, a flat
stain meshing the pile even flatter. I'd never seen it before
but I knew Michael made that stain. I knew all sorts of
things. What was under that the painted boards, the grit
between the slats. I could see things that weren't there. I
couldn't take my eyes off the white stain on the carpet.

132

David reached over and kissed me. I closed my eyes tight and tried to see only the dark. When he stood up, I didn't say anything. Not till I was sure he would hold me some more with my eyes closed. I wanted it too much to risk being wrong. Afterwards I cried till I screamed. I didn't know how much I needed to scream.

This is the pattern of what I do when I am with David. We get drunk and have sex and I scream a lot of the time. Michael's boots sit beneath my clothes on the rail in the corner of the room, David's jeans over the chair. He takes the screaming and holds me. I never scream any other time. In the early morning, he takes the car home for his father.

So. This is who David is.
    This is who David was.
I have problems with tenses. I have to remember things are not as they were because I have changed things. Knowing this would have to happen doesn't help. I form habits fast and break them slow and have no way to predict anything. I have no insight into his motives. I have no idea of what he thinks he is doing with me. Maybe now it has to stop.
I have to remember not to be dependent on any one person. David has insight into these things.

ooo

Mr Kaur's door is covered with writing again. NF and swastikas round the wrong way. Every other afternoon during lunch-time closing he scours things off. They reappear every morning. Mr Kaur cuts the string on newly-arrived colour supplements and says he won't be a minute. He says nothing about the graffiti.

Three or four of us stand around waiting. Somebody starts shouting up the end of the biscuit aisle. It turns out to be a fat man with an eyepatch, dunting his way past the granolas and shouting because there's no rolls left. What's he supposed to have for breakfast, eh? It's so loud the kids hanging round the door look in to see if it's a fight. He always has rolls. Always. What's he expected to do now? Mr. Kaur doesn't know. The fat man's face crumples. He rubs his jaw suddenly and asks for ten Players and five penny caramels. Afterwards, he stands just outside the open door, looking into the distance, astonished.

I walk back holding the papers into my chest to keep them out of the wind. I hate creased papers. Snapping the new pages gives me a thrill, like making the first footprint in new snow. Used to be the Post and the Mail, turn about between my mother and me till Myra woke up. Paul had his papers delivered. We branched out dangerously and tried the qualities: glossy supplements, review sections, etc. so there was a fair share of new bits, sides each on the carpet. Smell of fresh grounds, rustle of paper and no need to talk: all very cosy. By the time I got to the cottage it was habit. If I missed my paper I got moody. Michael wasn't much of a reader, but went out to hunt down an Observer to keep me happy. He had to hunt because it was afternoon before we were out of bed most Sundays. One day he was ages. I was frantic with pile-up fantasies by the time he got back. He'd been all the way to Troon to get the right one. Since he'd gone all that way he brought ice-cream as well. Strawberry. We went back to bed with the strawberry ice-cream and I read the paper at night instead.

ooo

Reading the business section, refusing to bake. The phone rings. David is subdued. He asks to come round and I hang up with enough time for a quick bathing ritual. It pays to be ready for any eventuality.

He arrives while I'm still changing, just a pair of jeans and

134

training shoes from the top of the stairs. The fair hair over the black collar. He shakes the car keys in his hand, the other crammed into his hip pocket and says Hi as though we're Lonelyhearts meeting for the first time. As though he isn't sure who I am. We don't kiss: we never do unless the kiss is safely sexual, outside any other interpretation. But I smile and run to the kitchen to make tea.

Put some music on, I shout.
Something we do in the evenings. After a moment or two *The Rise and Fall of Ziggy Stardust and the Spiders from Mars* floats through. He says he likes my records because they're so old. Joke. The volume is too low because it's afternoon and we're both on edge. When I pull the curtains, the room is too dull but the electric light is too artificial. I settle for half-open curtains and turn to the tea things nobody wants, pouring anyway.

So how was college this week? I sound like an aunt.
He pretends not to notice. Nothing exceptional. The usual. Went out on Wednesday with some friends. Nothing special.
I don't ask if the friends were a girl.

Exams soon? I say, stirring. Have to start studying in the evenings I expect, less time to yourself.
This amount of evasion is embarrassing. I'm scared to look up in case he knows perfectly well I'm providing escape clauses if he wants them. Maybe it's patronising. Teenagers can be so bloody touchy. He doesn't take the tea, just gets up to skip a track he doesn't like. In the middle of settling the needle back on the disc, he speaks, still with his back to me.

Don't you want to talk about hospital?
This is an effort to stop me asking questions about him.

Boring. There isn't much to say.
Oh?
He doesn't know any more than I do how far to push, how far he doesn't want to know. Old pals is the best tactic I can come up with.

You know me with strangers.
He sits again and looks at his nails. I know I ought to say

something negative. Negatives always sound like painful honesty.

It's impossible to see the shrinks. They're shut off all day in boxes and don't come out. I could wait all day and not see one. Then when I do I don't know what they're talking about.

Do they know what you're talking about?

I wait for a moment. I want to give him enough clues so he will feel sorry and touch me. I try to look stoic but hiding volumes.

No.

Whose fault is it? Are you telling them everything?

It's not the way you think it is. Not how I thought it would be either.

I'm talking too much. He is listening with his eyes unfocussed and I don't know what he's thinking. I never know. What I want to know is whether he's coming back to see me any more. This blocks most other things out. But I can't ask. These circumstances are not normal for us. We're not drunk: anything we might say is in cold blood. And all the need is mine. This is not a good position to be in. David picks at the rag-nail on his thumb.

Is it going to do you any good?

I smile and reach for the tea. I need a prop to pull this one off.

I have to think so. I have to try.

He wipes his forehead and the blues of his eyes show. I manoeuvre myself to the floor, leaning against his legs. A suggestion. He lets me lean there and we talk for two hours. We have plenty to say to each other about all sorts of things. Except what it is we are doing together. He reaches for my hand when he is ready to leave, offering a lift to Foresthouse as though there was no surprise in such a thing, as though it were our usual routine. All along the road I don't ask what I want to know. He waits in the carpark while I unbuckle the belt, having difficulties in the hope he will say something, tell me whether the sex is finished, whether we are Just Good Friends.

Can I visit sometime? he says.

That catches me unprepared. I say of course, I'd be grateful.

He kisses me outside the gates and I don't know what kind of kiss it is, what it means. Kisses goodbye are all much the same. He touches my shoulder but doesn't speak so I go inside not knowing. The red tail-lights are gone by the time I get through the revolving door. Nothing but grey in the window, the shape of my hand furring on the glass.

No-one else in the ward. I dump the holdall on the bed and listen for a moment to the movie drifting out of the dayroom across the corridor: people shouting, a helicopter take-off and gunfire. The ward smells funny. Maybe I smell like that too after a day in here. Maybe I just don't notice. I think about David in the car, changing gear along the shore road then tip out the holdall to get ready for bed. Nine thirty. A good girl stripping for my pink pyjamas and these bleachy sheets instead of David. The pyjamas look bloody awful. Tesco's: girls'aged 11. Terrible. But this can be a virtue. My renunciation of vanity. And it proves I'm trying. Blinded by the radiance of my gold star for effort, I dither into the corridor.
I forget.
I drop my guard.

You can't wait about in here like that.
At first I can't work out who's speaking. Then he comes closer: a white face and a white coat.
Are you listening? You can't wait here.
I say What? in a little girl voice, hoping for the best.
You heard me. You know you can't wait here like that. Come on now. Go and get your dressing gown.
What? I say. This is like talking to Myra.
I'm not having you standing here, he says. Not like that. He gives me a long look. You're not allowed like that.
The face looks as though it could be in my Third Year class; freckles and a faint ginger down on the upper lip.
It's not fair on the men. Get your dressing gown. You can't wear those tight things in a mixed area. Go on.
It has to be a joke. I look at him and know it isn't.
I haven't got a dressing gown.
You'll just have to change then, won't you?

I let him wait a while.
Yes, I say.

I can still be very good when I have to.

> *There are split seconds in the morning between*
> *waking and sleep when you know nothing. Not just*
> *things missing like where or who you are, but*
> *nothing. The fact of being alive has no substance.*
> *No awareness of skin and bone, the trap inside the*
> *skull. For these split seconds you hover in the sky*
> *like Icarus. Then you remember.*

ooo

There are no dreams in 1D.
The drugs are effective.

Colours come with the morning bell at 6.50.
No-one sleeps in. It wouldn't do to miss anything.

The men are always first in the breakfast queue, hiding
behind the smoke-screen. They carry their own ashtrays.
Mrs Marshall is up and running, doing her rounds in
sandals, print frock and no make-up while the old ladies of
1F blow bubbles onto their milk, splashing already cheesy
housecoats. Mrs Marshall ties on the last of the bibs, spoilt
for choice as the old ladies turn their attention to the food.

Mrs Marshall is English.

Open wide, Mrs Simpson. Open wide.

The accent cracks eggshells from the other side of the room. Mrs Marshall is a voluntary auxiliary. She comes here from choice to spend the day pushing puree between reluctant gums, recycling the drips with a plastic spoon. She never feeds Mary. Mary took a pot-shot at Mrs Marshall last year and broke her nose. Ros told me. Before long, she'll say, Well I can see I have my work cut out for me today! All pained reasonableness. She says it every day. I hate it but listen for it all the same. The dining room is a place for this kind of thing: the near-sexual thrill with the food and the dribbling old women, the random men. Everybody coughs. I am woozy and unhappy but I am not alone. We share each other in the morning because we have no alternative. No-one is allowed to sleep in.

Well I can see I have my work cut out for me today! Open Wide.

Grapefruit segments fresh from the tin and my first cup of coffee. The allowance is two cups but I take anything up to six if I can get away with it. Ros is already filling out her lunch card. I don't know how she can face it: the room stinking of blood pudding and weak kipper while she tests her appetite for lamb curry, spaghetti carbonara, stroganoff with noodles.. Christ, liver and onions. I take my card and tick salad. I always tick salad. Then Ros eats my grapefruit segments and we sip coffee waiting for the trolley to come. We all wait, in on the same joke. We have been woken up to take sleeping pills/ anti-depressants/ tranquillisers/ suppressants. But we don't mind. We wait good-naturedly because we don't know any better and because the pills work. It takes a long time for the overnight build-up to dissipate. John salutes when he knocks back the plastic cup. Ex-army. Twenty-eight going on fifty. My second week already and I know the names, little bits of history. I am learning the ropes/ getting the hang/ into the swim. Mrs Marshall knows to leave me alone.

The end room is always quiet. You can see the facing wall and a piece of visible sky. You watch it change colour.

What will I do while I'm lasting, Marianne? What will I do?

Notebook Magazines Needles   Wool   Notebook

Magazines Needles   Wool   Notebook Magazines

Needles   Wool   Notebook   Magazines Needles

Wool   Notebook   Magazines Needles   Wool

Spot the odd one out.
How many words can you make from the letters in 1D?

I-SPY WITH MY LITTLE EYE NOTHING BEGINNING WITH DR

Heat, changes in drugs and dosage. Things come and go and there are no divisions between. I try to record passing time. I make lists.

My Week by Joy Stone aged 27

MONDAY

A doctor came. A real one. Natty suit and a bowtie, long fingers. A gynaecologist. He wore no badge and didn't tell me his name. He asked if it was true I didn't menstruate. Dr Two must have told him our little secret. I admitted it straight out: It's true, I said. I don't menstruate. I gave it up to save money. I couldn't shut up. He prodded my stomach, unimpressed. Could I be pregnant? I laughed and he told me to stop being silly. I stopped being silly and acknowledged the possibility. Saying it made me sober up fast. He scowled even more and left without saying goodbye.

140

Visitors. Times are every Tuesday and Thursday but I took it for granted I'd be safe. Then Geraldine hunted me down in the end room. She knew exactly where I'd be.

Allan and Tony stood at the end of the white tunnel when I came out, pasty under the striplight. I wasn't wearing make-up.

I said, What are you doing here? What are you doing here? I wasn't wearing make-up.

Just up to see you, just up to see how you are, Allan said but he knew it was a mistake. Tony's teeth were yellow.

Just a visit to cheer you up.

They didn't stay long. After, I felt no better. I knew it would happen again.

Six of us followed Nancy in a ragged crocodile to the lift.

Woopsadaisy.

She always gets butterflies when it starts to move. Nancy is enthusiastic: she is an Occupational Therapist. The six of us followed her to the sewing room, soothed by her credentials. She gave us a cardboard box. The cardboard box was full of jumble. The jumble was part of the clothing store for long-term patients. Our part was to look for things needing buttons to sew them on. She had the buttons in her pockets: brought them specially.

Nancy has big green eyes and knows what's what. She asked if I was married and her eyes rounded when I said no. She said Never mind, then showed us all her engagement ring. She said it was best to use request sheets for presents: that way you avoided getting two of something, or rubbish you didn't really want and didn't go with your colour-scheme anyway. She saw them in Brides magazine. We sat in the sewing room surrounded by coloured rags not needing buttons. John tried on a woolly hat and Nancy said we were making a mess. We're worse than children.

Hello Dr Two.

Dr Two remembered me. I remembered Dr Two. No, there

was no sure way to make appointments. I had to understand they were very busy. People tended to make appointments for themselves if they felt they needed them. No he wasn't sure how long it would take yet: that was rather up to me.

THURSDAY
I took no chances. I washed my hair and put on some mascara. Anybody might come. David came. He waited at the end of the corridor and didn't take up my offer of a guided tour. I got two coffees and drank both. His lips were chapped. He told me it had been snowing. I told him I wrote to Marianne. He said he hadn't written yet but he would. He hadn't shaved. The occasional tiny bristle caught the light. I decided not to tell him about the gynaecologist. But I knew I should be thinking about this thing properly. While he was talking, I saw myself looking at babygros and feeder cups in Mothercare, wearing a dress with a pussycat bow in front. It was OK till I remembered about the bump and broke sweat thinking how fat I'd get.

So, I said, what have you been doing?
He'd been swimming at the weekend he said. Needed the exercise. A blond nurse about his age walked past and he let his eye follow. She rang the bell.
At the top of the staircase he said, I'll come on Saturday. Saturday, if you're home again. OK?
He didn't kiss me goodbye.
The blond nurse asked if he was my little brother and I said no.
She waited for more.
He's a friend. A good friend. Just a friend.
I knew I was blushing.

FRIDAY
I haven't written anything for Friday yet.

Some things are harder to pin down. They are not events but they happen all the same. I learn rules, givens and procedures. How to get extra drinks out the coffee machine.

142

Where they keep the spare towels, where there's less smoke, where it's quieter. Sometimes I walk for miles into town and stay in the shops where it's warm and no-one will talk
watch me eat
give a damn

where there's no danger of people getting too

I wanted to keep my distance. People can be so unpredictable. I have no insight when it comes to people: just a layer of missing skin. I never see things coming.

A man turned up at Ellen's door, someone I knew vaguely, shiny and eager to help out. He came for Norma. I asked why she didn't come herself and he laughed. HAHA. It was the kind of laugh that said everybody knew but me. Also he was nervous and upset underneath all the bluff. Anyhow, he wanted to look round the house in Boot Hill. I didn't question: it didn't occur. Since I knew his face I thought it would be OK I took him to the house. He went through bundles of Michael's things, the legal documents jumbled up with love-letters and petty erotica while I sat there, occasionally giving me things to hold. I realised later these were the ones I was being allowed to keep. At the time, I hadn't a clue. I thought I was helping. When he asked for the keys, I gave him the keys. I thought he knew best. It was only when he asked for Michael's ring that I ground to a halt. I said no. Nothing less than hand to hand. I would give it to her myself.
He smiled like a priest. Surely I didn't think she'd agree to that? Surely I knew why that wasn't possible?
I didn't know.
   Oh come now. He kept on smiling.
   What's the problem? I said. Don't you think we have a lot in common?

Norma showed up three days later. We were just two women talking together in a room. I handed over the wedding ring before we did anything else so she didn't feel she had to ask. Some other bits and pieces. The talk was

143

pretty stilted till she started to talk about the way he would never tell you right out what he was doing half the time. Once he put a down payment on a motorbike when they were just married without telling her. Of course, she found out then pretended not to know so he could keep his secrets. Some people need secrets. I told her he'd done just the same thing when he moved into the cottage and we laughed together. Then she realised what she was doing and asked for her coat.

On the doorstep she paused and turned round.

There's something I'd like to know, she said, and waited. Now I saw her in the daylight, her eyes were swollen.

You don't need to answer.

I said, Ask if you want to. It was my invitation.

It took her a minute to frame the words.

When did it start?

We both knew exactly what it meant. There was no mistaking. I also knew it didn't matter a damn. It was nobody's business but mine and it was also irrelevant. But I answered. I knew I didn't want to but I answered. Twelve forty-five. The lunchtime bell through the cello cases, the scent of rosin and used guitar strings, yellowing copies of Scottish Melodies. I answered down to the minute. Maybe I thought I owed her something.

She was looking at the square of old paintwork under the numbers I'd taken off, running her finger along the join.

I just wanted to know.

I was getting a creepy feeling in my stomach. Why? I said. What difference does it make?

She looked straight at me then.

Just that he would never tell me. I used to ask and he would never tell me. At least now I know. You told me something he never would. At least now I know.

I wasn't sure why but I felt I'd made the biggest mistake of my life.

A day or so later Marianne and I called to collect mail. The house smelled different and Michael's jacket was missing. Someone else had my keys. The place I lived wasn't my home any more. A lot of things got worse after that. My own fault. I never see things coming.

But you learn despite yourself: the names by absorption, the temperaments by feel. Through the layer of missing skin. I don't talk much but I learn nonetheless.

You learn
Ros and Norah. Janey with the sixty-a-day cough and the voice like lighted sparklers. Kathy's lumpy skin like leftover pudding, the baby she can't hold. Violet and Fat Betty have ECT. Mrs McQueen never knows where she is. Linda trailing around like Ophelia, calling for her father. John salutes. I try to learn nothing but pieces go in. I recognise faces and they recognise mine. What else filters through I have no idea. Staff are indiscreet. Nassim broadcasts my hiding place in the end room, Tom announces my job as a joke. There's no telling what else.

Tom came to get me on Friday morning. No appointment card but I had an appointment. He waited outside in the blue and white Maternity bay. I went further in. The gynaecologist had his own office, a sink where he scrubbed up in a sleek double-breasted suit, a white flower in his lapel. Wedding clothes. He said hello and sit please. Busy.
I waited under the lamps till he was ready, trying not to think what would come next. It wasn't much. He wanted me to take off my shoes and belt, work my shirt loose. That was all. I made myself accessible and slid onto the couch, crushing the neat paper sheet. My jeans weren't loose enough. I eased them back, watching those long sterile fingers ease into gloves.
    No sign of bleeding yet?
I shook my head.
    A scan is the quickest way to resolve things then. Best to be sure.
I agree it's best to be sure.

The gel was freezing but I didn't flinch. Then the monitor flickered and we turned to watch TV. The metal magnet was cold, drawing over the gluey stuff on my skin then sparks scattered on the screen, green splinter patterns like fireworks in a night sky. He frowned. I tried to see what he saw. This green cave was me. I make light on the screen therefore I am. I tried to lie back and see my insides objectively while the gynaecologist rubbed infinity signs over and over again on my belly. It wasn't swollen but so what. Maybe I really was pregnant. We might be doing more than discovering I exist: someone else might exist in there too. I scoured the screen looking for something sure to surface out of the haze on the monitor. The doctor stiffened.

Ahh. he said.

I stopped breathing.

Much as I thought. Nothing there at all. You can see for yourself. Look. You can see for yourself.

I looked. I was still there. A black hole among the green stars. Empty space. I had nothing inside me. The doctor smiled directly at me for the first time.

Nothing for either of us to worry about then. Nothing at all.

Tom held my arm and said nothing on the way back upstairs. He knew, though. I knew he knew.

FRIDAY

Still nothing to write.

The piece of sky through the scaffolding is navy blue.

Notebook Magazines Needles Wool Notebook

I look out of the window till Nassim comes.

On you go. No amount of telling with you. There is nothing to see out there. Now shoo. Go to the dayroom. They're playing Scrabble. Good game for teachers.

High summer. Flat blue sky spills upward from the dip between the hills but there is no air. The close sweet smell of earth baking in the heat.

Graves have two sides, runnels along the trench. Lots of people stand at the other side and no-one speaks.

Familiar brass initials on the side of the coffin sink. There is a seal round the wooden rim. I think what is sliding on the padded satin. What is still to come.

Sean holding my arm.

We wait in the car, stifling in the heat till the others leave, the plastic at my back drawing sweat. When there is no-one else, we cross to the cordon, the flowers in a pile. The sheen of varnished wood from the hole in the ground.

I know the waiting isn't over yet. There is always something not taken into account. Something more to come.

My first restless night in Foresthouse, the night-nurse gives me a little extra something to make me less anxious. I have bad dreams, I'm scared they get worse.

Silly, she says. No sense worrying over silly things. When my head is clear I know she's right.

There are no dreams in 1D. The drugs are effective.

Colours come with the morning bell at 6.50 then we dredge out of bed and follow the leader. No-one sleeps in. I know the names, little bits of history. I am learning the ropes. Mrs Marshall knows to leave me alone.

ooo

I had a recurring nightmare when I was small.
I was grown-up in this nightmare, waiting at a familiar stop for a bus. The stop was on the corner of two right-angled streets near the town centre. I would feel money in my pocket and watch the road. When the bus came, there would be subtle changes in the atmosphere of the dream. I would notice them vaguely but no more. After I'd been on the bus for a short time, though, I would get uneasy. The shelter was supposed to be blue. Why did I recollect orange? And the two streets. What I remembered now was open countryside. Greenish-grey grass in clumps and a dirt track, low light in the sky. This feeling would build up slowly till it broke all at once and I knew I was on the wrong bus. As soon as I knew for sure I saw there were no other passengers. Through the smeary windows, bits of somewhere I didn't know were hurtling by far too fast for safety. When I flicked my eyes to the driver's mirror, there was no reflection. No-one was driving the bus. As soon as I knew for sure, the bus got faster. All I could do was hold onto the seat rails in front as the acceleration got worse and the tyres bumped off the road and onto rougher ground. The bus knew where it was going even without a driver. So did I. There was a wall ahead. We were accelerating towards the wall and it was entirely my fault. I had got on the wrong bus. In the second of impact, I woke. This morning, it wasn't money in my pocket but pills. Enough for the weekend, loose. The first bus was fine. It was OK. Then about five minutes into the journey, I got this creeping feeling in the pit of my stomach. The bus wasn't

going the right way. It was turning off the main road and down some road I didn't know at all. I looked round the bus and felt better because all the people were still there. The driver's mirror was fine. I held onto the seat rail in front just to be on the safe side. Two little towns went past between big stretches of furrowed field and wild grass. More people got on. At the third town, there was fuss when an old man with a hearing aid the size of a brick got on and didn't know where he wanted to go. He just stood there, holding out his hand for a ticket and not saying anything. Once or twice he shook his head but he didn't hand over any money. He just didn't know. The driver let him stay but he got up at the next stop, moaning. A girl with a baby helped him off. Maybe he went around all the time like that not knowing where he was. A couple of stops after, I noticed some red high rises, a place that could have been the bakery. The middle of Boot Hill came up into view when I thought it would. It was just a different route. We must have stopped outside the cottage and I hadn't even noticed. Things had started getting familiar again and I hadn't even

A blue envelope.
Inside are six photographs of water and hills. Two have people I don't know holding up big flat wooden paddles. One has lots of sky and a white dot wearing shorts. Waving at the camera.

Dear Joy,
It's so good to get your letters. Well, maybe not good in view of what's in them but you know what I mean. Foresthouse sounds like hell. No it doesn't: it sounds like the staffroom. I think you'll last.

The photos are to show you what I do at weekends. A couple of the people I work with were going canoeing and I went too. We stopped off someplace called Montebello (Waltons country) and I got lost in a longrifles museum. The owner took a shine to me and played me and showed me this Appalachian dulcimer he made himself out of curly maple wood. He played me Danny Boy because he thought it was Scots. It was a good try. He wouldn't let me take any pictures though. He said if I came again he would let me try out one of the rifles. The canoeing place wasn't nearly as wild as the last one except raccoons ate my Cheerios in the middle of the night. Or maybe it was possums - anyway, something thorough. The last night I sat watching the sun going over the edge of the river and thought how different it looked. The Blue Ridge Mountains. Like the colours are slightly changed or something. The air too. It was really peaceful, just the sound of the water and leaves. Sometimes I wonder what the hell I'm doing here. I bought a bushel of apples and home-packed molasses. I don't know what you do with molasses.

Yesterday I went to a football match. Like Androcles and the Chess Board. The band were the best bit. They take the Stars and Stripes so seriously: marching, playing, flag-waving and all the rest. This after a day teaching the sonnets. Nobody was very pleased when I said 126 of them could have been written with a man in mind. Then I went home and baked banana bread and brownies. If you think of anything clever to do with molasses, let me know.

Today I taught three classes, rushed off to give a talk about Country Dancing (ridiculous) then came back and had turkey dinner and Pina Colada cake the Afro-American club were providing on a bake-sale basis. In the evening, I went back to college to wrestle with the xerox machine, finalise a report and copy out hundreds of terrible two-word-answer tests for a class. I have a million papers to grade in my office and instead I am writing this. Someone went by the window on a motor-bike and I couldn't work for a while. I only remember every so often. Then nothing is very real at all. Take care of yourself. Send me a photo as proof.

Lots of Love, Mxxxxx

Punching slips all day knocks holes in me. Allan doesn't mention the visit. Nobody else does either. I go to see Ellen and don't stay long which is just as well. The phone is already ringing while I'm fishing out the front-door key.

Hello *Hello*
All I hear is my own voice coming back. Nothing else. I think maybe I didn't hear because my heart is thumping in my ears from running.
HELLO *HELLO*
There's a noise of running water down the wire.
I shout HELLO *HELLO*

Hi *Hi*
A tiny voice comes through the sound of running water.
HELLO *HELLO*
Hi *Hi* It's David. *It's David*
Listen, there's something wrong with your phone *with your phone*
I shout I KNOW *I KNOW*
He says Can I come round tonight? *tonight night*
Sure *Sure* I'd love to see
WHAT? *TO SEE WHAT? WHA*
YES. *YES*
WHAT?

A big snakeline of YES cuts away when he hangs up, then I go through to the kitchen and switch on the immerser. I take two polaroids of myself facing the bedroom mirror. They dry on the window sill while I change the sheets.

The heartbeat gets louder. I roll closer to the sound,
tangling sheets between my legs, sticky with some-
thing heavy like honey.

If I open my eyes something terrible will happen.

Something works under the lids, trying to prize them
up.
I fight and win. The soreness ebbs away. Then in the
dark, someone reaches

warm fingers
enclose one breast and a shallow wetness sucks the
side of my neck. The smell of aftershave is overpow-
ering as his weight levers closer. Something like skin
brushes my

my breathing accelerates and

his mouth brushes mine but I kiss

> *nothing*

a cold place on my neck is all that is left of the melted
man.

My fault.
I opened my eyes.

ooo

THIS WEEK:
   OT (poetry)
   yoga and relaxation
   sandwich rota till Friday.
I have a full life.

I take the bus and go down town without asking. They never refuse me so I take advantage. Everybody does.
The corner church just off the shops has a new sign.

CHRCH THIS SUNDAY? WHAT'S MISSING IS U.

I walk past the church fast wondering what sort of people this is supposed to attract. I head straight for Marks and Spencer.

The morning after Michael's first official night with me, we emptied out the carrier bags and knew we would need to shop. Marianne drove round in the car and took us to Kilmarnock. Michael didn't know what day of the week it was and I was manic. Marianne took us straight to Marks and Spencer to look at the food. We bought some fancy pasta, tomatoes and a big trifle. Ginger biscuits covered with plain chocolate. After that, it didn't seem so bad. Every time he felt terrible again, he bounced the plastic bag to hear the biscuits rattle. He put his arm round me and jerked it away suddenly when he saw someone he knew. Forgot he didn't need to.

CHRCH THIS SUNDAY? WHAT'S MISSING IS U.

Kilmarnock is too busy. I already have Norah's black cigarettes, Kathy's coconut castles. I don't even know why Mina wants a bicycle bell. Halfords is empty. Just a boy at the back of the shop arranging a display of windscreen wipers. And me waiting with a bicycle bell. Someone comes in. The boy comes and takes his time with the till. He thinks the bell is the wrong price. While he checks through the catalogue I get a sudden whiff of aftershave. Leather creaks at the joints of a blue jacket. The boy's finger runs down a list of numbers and stops. The aftershave gets stronger through a familiar cough, then the click as his tongue flips a mint against his teeth. I watch my hand pay over Mina's money and take the bell. I leave without letting myself look round.

Moira gives me a row. I've not to leave without asking again. My lunch was ruined. Not only that but someone has been. There's a chunk of fruitcake wrapped in foil on top of my locker if I care to look. MUCH LOVE, ELLEN. I give the cake to Ros and feel terrible all night.

ooo

Dr Two's divorce still isn't through. We talk about his divorce. I tell him I keep waiting for something too but I don't know what it is.

Oh? he says.

Sure, I say. Half an hour before visiting times I change and put on make-up. I walk up and down the corridor and have to change clothes again because I sweat so much. The relaxation tape says to rationalise, be grateful. I can't be at peace.

He looks thoughtful. The half-hour is up.

ooo

Dear Marianne,
I have been feeling bad and not able to write. Tonight is a little better. Thanks for the photographs. I have one on my locker. You seem to be meeting a lot of new people.

My own new circles are more narrow, but I'm getting used to it. I wrote to school but no reply yet. I joined the yoga group and the poetry group. I don't like either of them but they might get me brownie points for trying. The poetry group is worst because they're all things I've used in school. Automatic pilot is never far away. Everybody gets bored with the poetry and talks about their dinner or operation scars instead. You're right: it's just like the staffroom.

I'm getting worried though. Some of the things I do worry me. I want things I can't have, trivial things. I want cards. I want cartoon characters and trite verses wishing me well. I see Michael in buses and cars and walks past the road outside the window. Visiting times are terrible. I can't get the hang of not wondering what to knit him for Christmas.

My hand is stiff. It's always chill in the end-room compared to the rest of the wing and my hand is cramped from writing too fast. I write too fast and dig the pen too hard into the page. I flex my hand and check the tone of what I've written. It needs a little something.

Dr Two tells me he has been talking to his colleagues. They were agreed about one thing. I am definitely depressed. It could be chemical or reactive or both. He plumps for the latter but it's hard to say. That was the good news. The bad is I am to stay for another fortnight. At least. I'll do as I'm told because he is a professional and I have no better ideas. Increasingly, I have no ideas at all. I get the feeling something is about to happen. Something scary. I am impatient and anxious but that won't make any difference. It will come in its own time.

The photograph you asked for is enclosed. I'm sorry it looks so terrible: polaroids never show me at my best.

I write HAHA so she knows it's a joke to be on the safe side then look at the photo near the edge of the table. I took it facing the mirror because I couldn't work the self-timer. The camera bludgeons off half my face and the flash whites out the rest. My arms are looped over my head to reach the shutter and hold the thing in place. It looks like a spider devouring a light bulb. The only visible eye is shut from the glare. It doesn't look like anybody. It doesn't look like

Outside there is scaffolding and a strip of moon. Pockmarks of rain on the glass. Alter the focus and you see eyes. They blink when I do but it proves nothing. There's no way of telling if it's really

Last Sunday night, I stole cards from the men's ward. There were a lot when I went past, just inside the ward door on top of someone's locker. Someone with a lot of friends. I lifted three and walked out with them under the waistband of my jeans then read them in the toilet where it was safe. *From Bob and the boys at work. Get well soon. Love to Uncle Charlie from Jean and family.* I tore them into confetti and buried them under peelings and wet tea-leaves in the kitchen bins.
I don't know what I'm doing any more. I look myself in the eye and see nothing I recognise.

The gum on the envelope sharpens my appetite. Soon the sandwiches arrive for supper with the evening coffee. Then there will be the night-round and the next day, the weekend. At the weekend I work with Tony and Allan and Mr Poppy. Allan will tell jokes and Tony will say I look well. We will all pretend together to be ruthlessly cosy. Then I will go home and wash my hair, scrape away the hospital and the punters'smoke, brush my teeth till the gums bleed
then

I like routines. You can get cosy in a rut. You can pretend things are the same when they're not. Knowing I need to live with lies makes me more anxious, depressed and guilty. This way I need the routines more.

Scaffolding and a strip of moon.

The edge of the motorway.

On Saturdays, David comes. We drive down the orange ribbon of motorway lights, the scatter of orange rain in the rear view mirror. I never ask where we're going. David comes back and we
pass gin from mouth to mouth

Three days till Saturday.

I know things have to change but not this week. Not tonight.

Not yet.

ooo

Rationalise, be grateful.
I put on make-up then sit just so on the topsheet of the bed, arrange the crease in my jeans, hold the crossword book, stare at the glass. Mhairi comes with sherbet bonbons. I hardly know her yet she lets me sit saying nothing for half an hour and leaves without a word of reproach. Three Fifth year girls next. Geraldine brings them through and they call me Miss Stone. They bring me a box of cakes. Everybody brings things. It gives them something to do with their hands. They tell me I'm thin, not sure if it's OK to say that to the teacher but I'm just the ticket/ pleasant as pie/normal as pinstripe. As a nine-bob note. They call me Miss. When they leave I hide in the end room till Tom comes to get me. I am not co-operative.

ooo

Our True-Life Dramas.
Tough Talking from Women who've Made It.
Post-natal Depression: The Secret Women Try to Hide.
I write Perseverence Makes A Difference.

ooo

Perseverence Makes A Difference.

Next morning it looks trite. The pen pokes right through the paper when I scour it over with ballpoint ink. The impression of repeated scores carries through for six pages.

Things to wash go in the holdall. Knickers and socks. The spare jersey. Nassim asks if I'm doing something nice tonight, funny look on his face. I never know when he's joking.

On the way out something caught my eye.

> **Janey**
> **Betty**
> **Ros**
> **John**
> **Phil**
> **Mina**
> **Me.**

GOODWILL INN: dinner with wine

An outing. Jesus. We're going out.

I just kept on going to the pharmacy with my head racing.
Dinner with wine. I didn't question: it didn't occur. I assumed they would have their reasons. Maybe you didn't
have to go. Then again, maybe it was therapeutic, like the
party. A therapeutic dinner with wine. Christ.

ooo

Mr Poppy had flu. Tony said I was looking off-colour and
I should eat more, it was good for my health. He winked
when he said it, as if he knew something I didn't. Maybe this
meal out was a joke. Maybe the ward staff made it up to see
who would fall for it and everybody knew but me. Allan
gave me a funny look.

I said nothing to David, whether he thought it was a joke or
not. Even falling down drunk I didn't say.

But I razed the house on Sunday. There was a black dress
crushed at the back of one of the cupboards, still talcy along
the seams from some other thing. I washed it in the kitchen
sink and packed it. Hidden under vests.

The first thing I did when I got back was head for the laundry
room for a towel I didn't need.

GOODWILL INN: dinner with wine

It was still there.

159

ooo

Ros wriggles into a long tube of blue satin. It's too tight but she doesn't care: it's nice to get dolled up, she says: feel like a woman again. Norah sits on the edge of her bed and tells her she looks knockout. Last week she didn't speak to us after she found out her name wasn't on the list. Now she is chatty and Ros looks a million dollars.

Ros smiles but there's something uncomfortable at the edges of her mouth. She swivels two cartridges of lipstick out of the barrels and asks for advice: Perky Pinky or Sunset Siren? What do we think?

Norah brings out a gold case and says, Here take mines. On you go. Dear stuff as well, out of Arnotts. Not cheap rubbish.

Ros hesitates.

Honest, Norah says. I don't want it any more. I'm leaving.

She draws coolly on a cigarette in the silence.

Tomorrow. So I won't be needing it.

Ros takes off the tight blue dress and folds it into her locker. She doesn't try on the lipstick. Norah sits on the edge of the bed, filing nicotine off her nails.

ooo

GOODWILL INN: dinner with wine

Janey is alcoholic/schizophrenic
Betty is afraid of everyone/chronically indecisive
Ros is a doormat/hormonally imbalanced
John never speaks/salutes
Phil is violent/alcoholic
and Mina.

I don't know who Mina is. I don't know what's wrong with Mina. Me. I can't figure out why I'm on the list. What's wrong with me.

At the meeting, Ben says he wants everyone to make an effort. We get leaving times and an assembly point. Like a firedrill. Betty isn't coming but we're not to worry. I worry. I have my dress and the strappy shoes. I have to lay hands on hairspray. Perfume maybe. Tights for godsake. I have to buy tights.

ooo

Nassim charges past the end room window twice and I slouch, trying to hide. I've made up my mind I can't go.

1. No-one will dance with me.
2. No-one will take me home.
3. No-one will play footsie/ hold my hand beneath the table/kiss me goodnight.
4. I will make no-one's evening.
5. I hardly know these people. We have nothing in common. We share nothing except sadness/ illness/ neurosis. We don't choose to be together. None of the things people come together for will be there.
6. The food, christ, the food.

Nassim charges back and spots me before I can get out of the way. He opens the door and looks.
Have you been here all this time?
I say nothing.
I've been looking for you everywhere, just everywhere. Hiding in here. I don't know what you do in here.
His face clears suddenly.
I have a surprise.
He smiles coy as the Mona Lisa.

Something came. Guess. I bet you can't guess.
I can't guess.
Look. The door swings out towards me. Look.
The rest of Nassim comes into view, brown arms spattered with white and pink. Flowers.
Secret Admirer.
He winks. The scent of carnations comes all the way across the room and makes me cough.

> Get Well Soon
> *TONY***xxxx**

Norah disappears overnight. The bed next to mine is unruffled. Her locker is open with nothing inside. No-one comes to take her place. I sit next to the flowers most of the morning and no-one moves me on. Instead they ask about TONYxxx and smirk. Geraldine says I should put a flower in my hair tonight, pin one to my dress.
Corsage, she says. That's what you call it. Corsage.
I tell her to take one for herself and disappoint. She wants me to be happy about going out tonight. The way she is. I should smile. She goes down the corridor whistling.

ooo

> A lot of astro-activity means it's time to sort out priorities: sure you're on course to get what you want from your current course of action? Could be a tense week. It's up to you to do something positive. The right attitude can move mountains you know! Romance is in the air from the weekend - get out and grab opportunities to meet dark strangers with both hands!

This is reassuring. It's not my fault if I have a terrible time this week: just the inevitable pattern of stars quite indifferent to me. Nothing personal.

Two interviews with soap opera stars. The older one says she was on the slippery slope to alcoholism but now she's happier and more self-assured. People just can't imagine the pressures and think it's all glamour. THE BEST MUM IN BRITAIN is a woman who fostered fifteen problem children in the past two years. The picture shows a huge woman with arms like white puddings hanging on butchers'hooks. Her eyes are huge. She says it wasn't her choice to be single but Mr Right never came along. Her arms wrap the children like bacon round sausages.

I write:
    You Should Count Your Blessings.
    You Have to Try.
    Laugh and the World Laughs with You, Cry and You sometir
                                                              get that
                                                              feeling

Moira appears suddenly in the middle of the philosophising and tells me Dr Three is wondering where I am. I am to come NOW. I drop the magazine and run like hell. The bus for the therapeutic dinner leaves in an hour and a half.

The *Argument before Couple go out to Dinner Party sketch*:
(a two-hander as seen on TV)
[Man is rushing to find bow-tie which is open around his neck. His specs are askew and his shirt-tail not tucked in. He wears only one shoe. Woman is drying hair and attaching one stocking to suspenders whilst applying lipstick. They look occasionally at watches and say O my god. Each blames the other for not being ready/ the fact that they have to go through with this charade at all and]
            NO NO NO NO NO NO NO NO NO
Just my little joke.
There is only me and Dr Three. He slackens off his tie to suggest a hard day at the office as do the piles of paper on the desk.

DR THREE	You forgot you made an appointment?
ME	No. Yes. Nobody gives me times.
DR THREE	Well, what is it on this occasion?
ME	[Trying to remember] Treatment. I've been here four weeks. I see different people every time.
DR THREE	Yes?
ME	I don't think I'm getting any better.
DR THREE	It doesn't happen overnight.
PATIENT	Dr Two said something about it last week. He said you'd have worked out some sort of treatment.
DR THREE	What sort of treatment do you want?
PATIENT	I don't know. What do you suggest?
DR THREE	Ah but that's the whole point. I'm not suggesting anything. You asked to see me and now you're just wasting my time.
PATIENT	[Hit where it hurts] OK. What about counselling? Or analysis? ECT even. How should I know?
DR THREE	Don't be ridiculous.
PATIENT	What am I supposed to do, then. Give me some sort of clue.
DR THREE	What does everyone else do?
PATIENT	They stop asking.
DR THREE	[Irascible playing indifferent] You can leave any time you know. No-one's keeping you here.
PATIENT	Look, all I'm asking is what use it's supposed to be, being here. I was advised to come. I want to know what for. I want help dammit.
DR THREE	You're getting the same treatment as everyone else. Rather better. You seem to get appointments with remarkable frequency. And there's no call for profanity.
PATIENT	But what good is this supposed to be?
DR THREE	Why don't you leave if you don't think we're doing you any good. Leave. Leave tomorrow if you like. I'll sign the form now.
PATIENT	You think I'm able to leave.
DR THREE	Certainly. Leave any time you like. Leave today. Get your bags and leave today. [This-will-teach-you-a-lesson]

164

PATIENT   [Inspiration] Dr Three? Are you OK?
DR THREE What? What? [Looks as though he's just lost
          something]
PATIENT   Are you OK? How's your head?
DR THREE How's what? [He looks childlike with confusion.]
PATIENT   Your head. I heard you get these headaches.
DR THREE Pah. [Face back to normal] My wellbeing is not
          your concern. Leave.
PATIENT   [Long pause] Why do you do this?
DR THREE I think this interview is finished. [Affecting cheer-
          ful dismissal] Goodbye.

[The patient waits, swaying. Slogans appear in the air above
      her head.
SERVES YOU RIGHT, YOU ALWAYS EXPECT TOO MUCH, etc.
Doctor pretends to read pieces of paper. They are upside
down. They fall on the floor. He pretends not to care.
Patient exits.]

You would think there's a natural limit to tears: only so
much the body can give at one sitting before it runs dry.

   This is no way to behave when you're going out.
Geraldine's hand presses into the mattress.
   Come on then. It can't be that bad. Tell me what it is.
   I rock on my side and keep my face turned away.
Geraldine gets distraught. She sends Ros to run a bath for
me. We have a bus to catch.

Hooks high on the wall. No lock.
Nothing sharp, no cords. The bath is plastic.
Heavy single drops squeeze from the tap mouth into the
yellow water. There is someone walking outside, further
away down the corridor. I watch the smoothness of the
plastic taps, the streaky pebble of soap. I watch my hand
reach for the soap and feel it slither on the whorls of
fingertips. It slips through the custard-skin surface of water
and enlarges. The ripples lick till they sear. I have lost the
ease of being inside my own skin.

165

I press against the plastic and let the water rise.
Time is not a healer.
I have lost the ease of being inside my own skin.

Separate streams cold and hot twine about my legs and over
my stomach; weaving the seaweed at my crotch. Cold rock
pools in my navel and between the breasts when I move. I
trace the hairline, the swollen jaw, the neck and breastbone,
the sour nipples, concave saucer of stomach. Nothing there
at all. I flatten my back against the bottom of the bath.

He must have been under the water for ten minutes,
maybe fifteen. That yellow bruise on his forehead
and the two on the chest: hit his head on the bottom
maybe. Did I have any reason to believe he did it on
purpose? Any reason at all?

The sound of heartbeat in my ears.
Low roaring of water.
And something thudding.

The lights come back too bright. Upright and choking for air
I hear Maureen knocking on the door.
Everyone's going to be late if I don't hurry.

Very pretty.

The black dress is too big, belted tight at the waist, bagging where my cleavage used to be. Eyes bloodshot under the purple shadow, lipstick fraying already. I look exhumed. But Dr Two says I am pretty, very pretty. Ros shows off her shiny blue, ankle bleeding where she cut herself shaving. John sweats through his cologne and white shirt and the other one is Mina. Mina wears a fur coat. Mrs Morrison thinks we look just splendid.

ooo

Ben in the foyer: stetson, silver tips on his collar, a bootlace tie with a skull pin. Howdy, he says and everybody laughs. He has the accent to a tee.

The lagoon room is turquoise with plastic waterlilies, the unmistakable stink of chlorine. Janey and Phil ask for tonic water with slices of lemon while Geraldine tells the waiter the mud isn't our fault: we had to walk from the bus stop. John is nervous too, watching other people at other tables being served hoping they are not watching us. A different waiter churns past to somewhere else. When the drinks come, they're in plastic glasses. Ha. They must have heard where we're from. Hahaha. It takes hardly any time to order since they're all starving. Two hours past feeding time. Plates come with the food attached and no need for the awkwardnesses of waiters hanging over our shoulders, wine in three bottles. Ben shifts the bottles nearer himself as a joke. This way they are further from Janey and Phil: professional touch. I chew melon as though it might explode, pick at the salad. I drink lots of wine. It has no effect. I need effects. Opposite my empty glass, Mina's fingers are lilac at the edge of the greying cast: her nails glossy and scarlet. Nobody asks what happened to her arm. Someone comes for the sweet order. Ros and Geraldine choose chocolate profiteroles with cream. The men all order ice-cream: nothing fancy. I order gin. Over dessert we talk sex, money, religion, family. There need be no taboos. We are all beyond the pale. We share adjoining wards. We share Dr Three. We have seen each other in other moods, other settings. A lot of people appear suddenly with the second round of coffee: the overspill of a works dance. I've danced with some of those men but none of them recognise me. It's Paul's works dance.

Every year I went with Paul to the works dance. I thought it was very grown-up: always wore an evening dress and took hours tarting before I was ready. My mother thought it was humorous. I don't know what you do to your face that takes that amount of time. Simple things.
The works always ran a bus because it was expected we would end up drunk. Some people took a carry-out on the bus and even started drunk. There would be a meal and some standing about, then dancing. Just like a wedding reception. Every year I would be introduced to Paul's workmates and shout at them through *Tie a Yellow Ribbon* or *Green green grass of Home*. Sometimes all the men would disappear and I'd be left with women I didn't know who in turn were left with me. Between times, you had to check the elaborate hairdo wasn't shelling kirbies and that your lipstick didn't look like you'd just eaten three tins of tomato soup. It made me feel like an escort girl only unpaid. Every year at the works dance, beery men would ask when we were setting a date and I would pretend to be deaf.
Now here we are again. Just like old times.

A Dynasty set builds up in the foyer but Paul is not among them. If he is here I want to see him first. At a table full of people I am lonely. I have no more wine. Phil leaves to go to the toilet and Ros follows. I pretend to follow her and order double gin at the bar. Downing the second, I see Phil and Ros in the bar reception suite. They kiss. I want to go back to the ward. The hollow echo and the smell of chlorine makes my head sore. But this is what there is now. I sit at the table with people I don't know and try to love them more. We are sharing the terrible minutes together. There must be something touching in that. There has to be something. John leaves the table fast, clipping my elbow. He's going to be sick.

The last bus running with lights low to avoid passengers has to stop. Mina stands in the middle of the road to make sure. Phil sings Bay City Rollers songs in the blacked-out back of the bus. Shang-a-lang is his favourite. Ros joins in. Janey gets out two stops before the hospital to get more cigarettes in a chippy. There is an off-licence at the same stop and she tells Geraldine she will walk the rest of the way. Geraldine rolls her eyes. She knows fine but says nothing.

The hospital is in darkness so we tiptoe, giggling and saying Ssshhhhhh because it's expected. The late nurse wants to shake her head and tut that we've had such a nice time. We don't let her down. She has the last laugh. No medication because we have been drinking. She shooshes too much and wakes some of the others. They turn under the blankets, grunting like seals in the wash of dark. The sheets are freezing. I curl up, legs against my palms. There is a silky rip of movement as Ros drifts out in her nightie to meet Phil somewhere, then Janey stumbling, the clink of cans. I breathe deep. No medication. I turn over the pillow, still damp from the afternoon, stifling my mouth with the hospital motif. It takes me so much time to learn the simplest truths.

This is the Way Things Are Now.

After half an hour, I ask the nurse for some mogodon to put me out. I am no stoic. The nurse is.
She doesn't give me any.

ooo

Tom arrives with the alarm bell.
He has a piece of paper and a holdall.
I'm leaving.

Within fifteen minutes Dr Three's private joke is annulled.
I wait in the corridor for the rest of the morning, listening
for his big flat-soled shoes. I want to look Dr Three in the
eye. I want to glare the bastard to death.

I wait all morning. He doesn't come.

ooo

Dr Two comes over while Ros and Kathy are eating sweet
and sour pork. Chatty. He asks if we had a nice night out.
   Yes, I say. Lovely. Bit like being trapped in an existential
novel.
Dr Two smiles a watery smile and hands me a book called
Courage and Bereavement. He looked it out specially. The
wrapper is purple with doves and clouds, warm and flaccid
from his inside pocket. I say thank you and feel sorry I
wasn't nicer about the night out. Ratepayers paid for me to
have this terrible time. I embarrassed Ros. Kathy doesn't
make judgements. She's into her second pudding.

I go back to the waiting area and write:
The More Something Hurts, the More it can Teach Me.

I feel this way I'm doing my duty by the ratepayers.

At last, the opportunity you've been waiting for. It's taken a long time coming but rest assured it's here for good. Let your heart rule for a change: some things do work out for the best, you know! Luck and love arrive in plenty in time for your birthday month. Keep smiling!

I sit some more waiting. He doesn't come.

Courage and Bereavement: coming to terms with death. **Chapter 1**: I will be shocked and angry. I am not to worry. It is normal to be shocked and angry. Plenty of people feel like this.

Chapter 2: I will overcome the shock and anger in time but not to expect anything to change suddenly. I will overcome my feelings of shock and anger if I take my time and give grief its own time to work through.

Chapter 3 says to get my family around me. My family will be a source of great strength and comfort if I let them. Blood is thicker than water.

Chapter 4 says to get my friends around me and talk. Talk. Remember the person as they were in life and the times they made me laugh. Laugh. Laughter is the best medicine.

Chapter 5 says to watch out for people who are avoiding their own embarrassment by trying to make me get better too quickly. I must expect some people to behave oddly. I may lose some people I thought were friends. Some men prey on vulnerable women: be cautious of too much sudden interest from men. It says never mind because I have my family and my real friends. This is a time for reassessment. I am not to be afraid of change.

Chapter 6 says to accept invitations and TRY. It says to take up people's offers of assistance and TRY. It says to buy myself little treats. It says to take up new hobbies and find myself. It says to go on holiday and discover things.

171

New surroundings can work wonders.

Chapter 7 says to speak to others in the same position and learn from what they have discovered. I am not to let myself go. I should watch my appearance and not be a source of worry. It says to read this book.

Chapter 8 says to talk to my gp. It says to talk to a priest or pastor or rabbi. It says to beware of alcohol and self-destructive behaviour. It says not to resort to tranquillisers or prescribed drugs. They do nothing.

Chapter 9 tells me stories of True Life Coping. It tells me I am not alone. The author tells her own story. Her brother died in a car accident. It took her fifteen years and three of psychoanalysis to forgive him. I should go into a warm room with someone I trust and get them to hold my hands. Then I must shout. I should shout all the anger out of my system. Then I should say I Forgive You.

American publisher. I should have known from the spelling.

Chapter 10 is a prayer. The author wishes me good luck.

I read the book in two and a half hours and cry all the way through.
Like watching Bambi.

ooo

The bus-stop looks nothing like the dream bus-stop. Not when you really look. Change for the fare bounces in my hand. I slip the bottle with my weekend allowance deep inside the bag and find my notebook.

I will Take Advice and Try Harder.
Expecting the Worst means Less Disappointment when it

Comes.
The More Something Hurts, the More it can Teach me.

I should refuse to see Dr Three again. He always makes things worse. My notebook will be better than a doctor. I have to learn to minister to myself and let the slogans teach me something. Maybe that was the idea all along.

I write:
Persistence is the Only Thing That Works.

I forgot to write:
Beware the Maxim.
Neat Phrases hide Hard Work.
Everything Worth Having is Hard as Nails.
I forgot there is always a price for forgetting.

ooo

Tony was in a good mood. I said thankyou for the flowers and he told me a joke:
Q. How many psychiatrists does it take to change a lightbulb?
A. One. But the lightbulb must really want to change.
He squeezed my hip when I laughed then told me I was too skinny.
Look, see? squeezing my backside: Nothing to hold onto. Thinking about that made him hungry. He fished out a poke of crisps from under the counter and unzipped them, leaning back to think. Maybe we could have a meal. Go dancing.
Tony, I said. Why do you never take your wife?
He looked offended.
She has her own friends, he said. She does all right.

I felt bad afterwards. No matter what I do, I usually feel bad afterwards. Look, I thought, Tony is not a bad man. He's being kind. I should accept kindness for what it is, do more

173

to help myself. And David has exams soon: he could do with
the time to study. I must not cling. I must accept invitations
etc etc. The callbox at the end of the road hove into view.
Tony said he would collect me at seven.

someti
presen
that st
before
late bu
ignore

Stars in the sunroof. His car smelt of cigars and aftershave.
I said, What age are you, Tony? getting used to smalltalk.
Making do. His teeth glittered under the moustache and
told me he was twenty-seven. He looked back at the road
and I looked at him. Camel coat and grey silk tie. Twenty-
seven. Christ. Same age as me. He patted my hand and put
on a Country and Western tape.

> *When you think I've loved you all I can*
> *I'm gonna love you a little bit more*

The waiter knew his name. Tony ordered a fresh bottle with
every course. I dabbed my mouth coyly with the napkin and
went to the ladies' after I finished eating. Tony was buoyant
when I got back. We went dancing.

often
the wa

He invited himself into the livingroom, sat on the sheet-
covered sofa flicking cigar ash into the neck of an empty
bottle. I didn't say no. His mouth over mine was warm and
made me lonely. The lips were warm but not full. They had
no surface. I would not sit on his knee but the kissing was
taken for granted. He had paid good money, after all. A
meal, dancing, flowers. It was Sunday morning.

ignore
warni

I forgot he doesn't drink coffee. I wasn't supposed to forget.
I said won't your wife be wondering where you are? and he
put his hand over my mouth. I turned my head and he kissed
my neck. I said I really think you should be thinking about
going now and he said Let me see where you sleep. I want

to know where you sleep so I can think of you there. I tried to laugh but I was too tired. He said I can't get you out of my mind. I think about you all the time. What does it mean? What does it mean? Something caught in my throat when he spoke. A spark of terrible anger that he should dare say things like this, expecting me to listen. A spark. I swallowed and said nothing. I made excuses. Maybe he thought women liked to hear this kind of thing.

warnings ₅
when the ₁
happens

I didn't pull back when he put his tongue in my mouth, stroked the nipples under the cloth. I gave in. I took him upstairs and showed him the bare boards and dust on the floor, the rail of black clothes, the single curtain. It didn't matter. He leaned into my shoulder and kissed my neck, tilting towards the bed, one hand slackening his shirt. I fell back as he spread out against me, pressing into the bone. His hands moved across my clothes lightly, like surgeon's gloves. No real substance. But I knew he was real. It was me who had no substance, nothing under the skin. When I spoke he covered my mouth again, cigar smoke in his saliva. The belt slid under my back. He couldn't find a way inside my dress. I undid the buttons myself to make it quicker.

worst hap₁
we can onl
blame

Is this what you want? I said. Will this keep you happy? He kissed me deeper and wouldn't answer. He pretended not to hear when I told him to put out the light. I did it myself, turning away from his face. He mistook the fractured breathing and moved heavier against me, angling my knees with his own. I was too tight: muscles clenched with crying, difficult to penetrate. But he persisted. Three snubbed strokes before he reached for his spit and I was easy as a rocking horse. He whispered, Tell me you like it when I come.

blame ours

Afterwards, he said he wished I had talked more. I should have spoken to him, said things. And shouldn't I stop crying now. He wiped himself down with his white handkerchief

175

and told me it was all right now. Stop crying. He sighed. He was better off the way things were before. He wished I would stop crying. When he was dressed he held me and said I would be all right. He said I would be fine after I'd had some sleep. I had too much to drink. I heard him lock me in, the key falling through the letterbox onto the concrete.

alone

ooo

Sunday Morning.

The square of wetness on the sheet follows me. I get up and wash in the half-dark. The empty glass near the bedside crushes against the woodwork, crackling like an electric charge. I bleed

feeling o

dozing on the damp sheet.

News and theological gossip, Pick of the Week, Desert Island Discs.

Downstairs, the garden is white. Coated in a fuzz of frost, like mould. Before we went to Spain, Michael went out and dug over the worst of the weeds with a spade, turning the earth with his foot: cold, slope-sided segments of cake. He dragged mud into the kitchen, walking across to me, something white curled in his palm.

Look, he said. Look.
A bird's skull. Bleached bone, the eyesockets clean. I should have looked at the hand beneath, the lines and signals. I should have looked harder. All I saw was the skull. He dowsed what was left of the ground with weedkiller, poisoning the whole patch. All that was left when I came back were sticks, rotted twigs poking through the clay. And a footprint, filled with rainwater. It could have been any-one's.

White winter light in my eyes, I make tea and try to sit still.
It's not Tony's fault. It must be me.
I make tea and try to stop shaking.

I don't want to be here. I want the morning old ladies and the ward light in my eyes, Ros and Geraldine, Nassim and Moira who don't give a damn. I want to unpick pieces from my head and not feel like this. You can't get away from the inside of your own head. Look, I am not a bad woman. I have committed no act of malice. But everything I touch turns bad. Christmas is coming and I have nothing to give. The house is dirty and sluttish. The outside drains are clogged with putrid apple pulp from the last time I made jam. I can't work out how to shift it. It gets worse every day.

The More Something Hurts, The More it can Teach Me.

But I want the end-room with the radiator too hot to touch and the rain outside, lights all day and night. The keys are cold from where they have lain on the paving, crawling with absent slaters and invisible atoms torn from Tony's hands. Outside slats are missing from the fence. I want to run.

ooo

Weeks follow weekends: patterns of fives and twos from schooldays. Really there's no such thing. Just passing time.

My father comes to see me. My father has been dead for twenty-two years but he makes the effort. Geraldine tells me he's waiting at the end of the corridor.
My father is wrapped up in a black coat as though it's cold in here. I'm wearing a polo neck. It could be a family trait. Then my father looks up and turns into Mr Peach but older. His skin is waxy and his eyes are pale. I don't sit down.
    How are you? is all he says for a while. He's not sure why he's here either.
    It's hard to find out, I say. Nobody will tell me.
He smiles uncertainly.
    I came to see how you were, he says. In case you harbour

any wrong impressions.

Wrong impressions?

About school. The service and so on.

Oh.

There's a pause where my teeth itch.

People make mistakes, he says. They can harbour wrong impressions.

Yes, I say. They can.

Neither of us knows what comes next. I stumble into Marianne in the Bue Ridge Mountains, menu cards, visiting times and Christmas coming soon, before he knows it I'll be back in my room at Cairdwell jings time flies. My mouth runs like a sewing machine. He looks at me as though he isn't sure whether I'm sedated properly then a horrible noise happens. Some kind of roaring out of the mouth of E block and Linda staggering out in her dressing gown. She stops and takes a look at us then starts wailing again. Mr Peach shifts in the seat next to mine. When I look round he's holding out his hand.

Hello Linda, almost whispering. She squints sideways, caught out.

Linda used to live next door, didn't you? he says.

She starts edging closer but not really wanting to, as though the hand might be a mine and blow us all to hell but must be picked up. It must be approached.

Long time eh?

He used to take her out in her pram, he says. I imagine a cartoon Mr Peach-as-young-man, grinning and pushing a big blue baby carriage. She's holding his hand when Tom arrives, apologising. She goes without protest. Mr Peach thinks he should be going too. I tell him to look after himself and he doesn't know what to do with his face.

I tell Geraldine he isn't my father and she says Oh.

Oh. Somebody came looking for you a fortnight ago too. After eleven. We sent her away.

She looks guilty but tells me the rest anyway. A strange woman and a man. They checked it out but I had no next of kin on the admissions form. Now who would it be?

I can't think, I say, not looking her in the eye. I can't
think.

ooo

Dear Marianne,
It's snowing. I have broken veins from the heat in here
and the cold outside and look like a Dutch Doll. The
picture of health. There was a lot of mail at the weekend: I kept your card. The other two were some legal
stuff and a builders' estimate which I burned. I am
slightly less invisible than I thought.

I'm not feeling too good right now. My birthday is
coming. Christmas is coming. I've seen three different
doctors in the past fortnight, none twice.
Dr Four says I need ECT, Dr Two thinks I need a good
holiday and a career move, Dr Three thinks I take too
much caffeine - a bit less and I'd be fine. Also a Dr
Five turned up and suggested maybe we could have a
chat. A CHAT. They increased everything sedative. This
means my hands and legs take me by surprise occasionally: I have to remind myself they are attached.
Yesterday Dr Four bumped into me in the corridor and
didn't know who I was. It struck me after as pretty
profound. Anyway, they think maybe I should stay a
while longer. This is probably what the anti-depressants are for.

A critical time is coming very soon. I have to think
about all sorts of things I can't bear to. I have to get
better. I have to get better because a) it'll stop other
people worrying about me; b) I'll stop being a drain on
the NHS; c) it has to be better than this. All theory,
however. I can't muster any faith in its being true.

I'm sorry these letters are always like this. Please write

and tell me what you are doing, how you pass the time
of day. And tell me jokes.

I manage *love* on the bottom after a struggle.

ooo

Hello.
The flat-soled boots pattering along the tiles under white
light. Still dark outside: daylight comes late and leaves early.
A white hand waves in the blacked-out glass.
My hand.
Mina comes along the corridor, flat on her back, smiling
lopsided with her face pale. Two men in white tunics
pushing the stretcher. Tom comes too. He is angry with
Mina and he won't speak. But I do. I say HELLO TOM
loudly, HELLO and watch him glare. Mina is due to go this
week. Mina is readmitted every time she is due to go. The
last time it was threatening behaviour that did the trick. This
time, a bloody wrist and two gashes on the upper arm. They
say Mina, why won't you go to Ailsa? They have more
doctors at Ailsa. This is not a long-stay ward. But they also
have better security at Ailsa and Mina won't go. This time,
they are going to take her there whether she agrees or not.
Her man won't be able to afford the fare to Ayr to see her.
But her smile stays on through the rattle of the stretcher on
the carpet tile, happy with the intravenous coils around her
wrist. She is too doped not to smile.

In the dayroom Mrs Morrison has a pretty cardigan and a
clean blouse. She has new slippers, a present from her grand-
daughter. She is sitting patiently today. She is getting her
hair cut in the dayroom by Moira from 4F. A treat. Her face
is flushed. But Mrs Morrison must be watched in case she
grabs the scissors. Her skirt rides up and shows her drawers.
She knows but doesn't care.

Stanley is a new boy. He stands in front of the TV, waiting:

the same place all week. The TV is not switched on yet but he waits there anyway. Stanley's scar no longer bleeds into his collar but the wound still seeps. It looks like a burst plum. He wears plaid shirts to hide the staining. His collar is always sticky. It glistens when he moves his head. He can't scratch his neck or the scab will tear. He twitches with his eyes closed and waits for the TV to start.

Violet wears a neat two-piece and matching blouse. She gives out books to the old ladies in their armchairs, making watery pleasantries and helping the staff collect ashtrays. Five weeks ago she drooled onto her dressing gown, shuffled along the corridor after invisible insects. She bit. Now she remembers nothing of this and is full of wonder when anyone mentions it. We all remark on the difference. The difference is ECT. Dr Four trusts ECT and now so does Violet. Violet goes home soon, friends with electricity.

I have a place on the sandwich rota. Geraldine shows me her nightschool essays out of faith I know what to do. Kathy speaks to me. Silent Kathy. Last week she asked me for a skirt.
    The father's coming the day, she said.
I didn't know if she meant her own father or the baby's father but I gave her the skirt. She burst the zip seam pulling it over her hips.
    It fits lovely, it's lovely, she said and went back to lie on her bed. Nobody came. She says how much she likes the skirt every day.

Ros's boyfriend says hello.

People know who I am.

ooo

Nancy arrives to collect us for OT. Today we paint Christmas pictures. The best ones might go into the children's ward, the one that is separated from our own with alarm-wire. This is unlikely since there are four weeks to go till Christmas but it's best not to make a fuss. Nancy frowns when I ask to draw, foregoing the poster colours and the crusty hoghair. But she gives permission. I get two sheets of paper and a warning not to ask for more. I draw

and nothing else.
I wanted to draw a landscape but it didn't come.

Nancy said What's that got to do with Christmas? I don't see what that has to do with the subject at all.

Isa makes a child's Christmas tree, coloured ovals balancing on the saw-tooth edges. Ros makes a brown splash between white and blue mashed potato. The the splash grows legs and a yellow beak. The red ellipse comes last. Robin in the snow she says: I'm no good at drawing. She tears it in two. Nancy tops up the paint boxes and tells us to be careful.

Janey, silly girl, she said. How will anyone know what that's meant to be. You've only done two. How many wise men are there, Janey? How many?

Janey walks away leaving her paints to dry out. I ask Nancy why she didn't get any of the men to paint Christmas pictures. She bristles.

I don't see what that's supposed to mean. Miss Pass-remarkable. If you're trying to stir trouble you can just forget it.

ooo

Norah's bed has been empty for days. Betty's for two. Kathy is being considered. More people go home near Christmas. There is a lot of pressure to get well, not to disappoint. Last

182

year we went to Ellen's. She gave Michael a knitted tie and Marianne gave him a big bolt of gold-coloured corduroy so we could cover his lousy sofa. Seventeen yards of corduroy. I thought he was going to cry.

Christmas is coming.
Two senior girls arrive with an invitation, a ticket to the school dance. Their cheeks are flawless, eyes round and white. I smile till my mouth frays, catch sight of myself in the glass panel over their shoulders and keep tight control of my breathing. When they go away I get hysterical. There is worse to come. I race downstairs with my purse clanking for chocolate and biscuits, driven by need I can't control. Chocolate and biscuits will not take it away but they are sweet and blot out everything but my mouth. For a little while. I eat as many biscuits as I have the money for and throw up in the space of fourteen minutes. Soundlessly.

Christmas is coming.
I pick up the sweater I'm knitting for David out of wool from something else and settle back in the dayroom chair. Mrs Morrison checks my pattern and tells me it's lovely, shrieking because she is deaf. She knits christening shawls all the time though she has no children. Two ply and tiny needles all day for no-one in particular. Ben and Moira rearrange the chairs till everyone gets a good view then the movie starts. ZOMBIE FLESH-EATERS. I pretend not to be watching a lot of it and stare at my knitting with my backside getting numb: the video scares me. It isn't the film so much as the men enjoying it so much. I daren't look at the old ladies. No-one asks what they'd like to watch. When it is over Ben puts on the news. Card schools break out the minute they recognise the tune. I hunt down the coffee machine and filch three in a row before I go to the kitchen to make sandwiches for the dayroom supper. Two kinds of bread. The old ladies are given white.

Q. How many psychiatrists does it take to change a light bulb?
A. One. But the lightbulb must really want to change.

183

No amount of sore throat or acid in the stomach makes any difference. My teeth are beginning to dissolve, dissolution of the enamel producing with the saliva a corrosive agent, the breaking up of the brain. Haha. Cavities shifting from one rightful place into somewhere they have no right to

One of the nurses hears me coughing up sandwiches in the bathroom and I shout through the inbreaths. Everything's fine. Jesus christ jesus leave me in peace. The petite blond with big eyes is there when I go out, hands behind my back. I smile too wide and get brittle, walking away sooner than is polite. I have to go to the end room.

I want to be held
   to be found

    not to think

     there is
     no going back only further
       going back only further

     jesus
     say there's nothing
     say there's

       jesus
       jesus
       on a grey table, eyes wide to the white light.
     His chest slack with yellow bruises where they tried
     to make the heart

     neck chain filled with water like fish eyes
     fingers tinged with blue

refusing to come back to
what was it?

the past tense made me

A uniform doubles back, opens the door and looks.
It goes.

I crawl out from under the window seat but cramp makes
me limp and a junior arrives too soon. He is a stranger. Dark
skin, white coat. He talks in a practised monotone until I
stop shaking. He is calm and nice to me. I can't look him in
the eye but he lets me sit, sharing the silence with me.

He says maybe I want to speak about

> *an ante-room after a lot of opening and closing*
> *doors. It felt tight and enclosed after the corridor,*
> *too full of people. The doctor made signs with his*
> *hand and an olive-skinned boy, about sixteen or so,*
> *came out from the middle of the huddle of white*
> *coats. I was saying Tell me he's all right, Tell me he's*
> *all right, not able to stop. The Spanish boy reached*
> *out his hand.*
> > *What was his name?*
> > > *jesus*

His voice came through everything else, finding my
language. You must be still. You must try to be still.

The only thing you can do is be still.

I didn't even thank him.

I look up at the junior and he looks back, waiting.
  I say, I didn't even thank him.
He nods.

The uniform puts me to bed. Before long the teeth are
rattling again. Chittering of the teeth that shakes the bed
and makes you get up and out of this bloody thing it
starts again

it

starts
again

              especially for his   *wife*

           especially   his wife

when you're in
love with a beautiful woman   *sometimes i get that*
it's hard   *feeling of*
            your cheatin heart
              will tell on
                                        you
        There is something more to
              something more

       when you think I've loved you all I can
    There is always something
                    more
                        to COME

throwing off the
sheets and searching, raking through a spill of make-up bag,
magazines, paper and pens. Pills are missing. A special
collection over weeks and someone has taken the pills. The
nurse comes, the Irish one with the face like fizz and wheels
my locker away, returns with a full needle the bitch the

186

bitch. Watching the blue ward light makes white rails across
the aisle, the sound of wheels outside. Janey moaning in her
sleep creak of springs while the drug
      snakes cold
          up the length of
                    an
            arm

My arm.

It's dawning on me where I am.

oops

The cap seals break one by one under the tissue. Pink tissue. Next to the glass, the chunk of paper bag that is my weekend shopping. The glass rocks on the cushion of my lip till it warms and the fumes burn my nose. I lift the glass again, toasting the card on the half-made shelves.

Happy Birthday.

I got:
two bills
a Christmas card from an Indian Restaurant
a letter for someone who doesn't live here
and a card from Marianne. George Washington staring from the stamp unable to tell a lie.

> Dear Marianne,
> I'm home for my first long weekend. A tryout. I don't know what to do with myself. I don't know what to write.

Self-conscious. I'm looking over my own shoulder, watching the pen in my hand writing monstrous

When I was a teenager, my mother use to go looking for my diary. I'd find my underwear rearranged, too neat and know. Sometimes she would find something she really liked and bring it into the livingroom as a surprise, recite bits for Myra's benefit while we were watching TV. I was too stupid to stop writing. I just took to hiding it in harder places. She kept finding it. One day what she read made her burn it. When I came home she showed me the ashes and said I could never be trusted again.
Paul read my diary as a matter of course. I shouldn't be afraid to leave it lying around casually because we had no secrets. Paul didn't keep a diary. A few months after he noticed it wasn't quite so available he hunted it down. He never actually said I couldn't be trusted again or deserved all

I got: it was taken for granted. When I moved to the cottage
I kept a red diary as big as a roadmap by the bedside. But I
couldn't work out who I was writing it for any more. Whole
weeks got missed out. Whole months. After Michael moved
in, there wasn't much time for writing. I threw the diary
away. His own diary was indecipherable. He wrote it in
code.

Dear Marianne,
I'm home for my first long weekend. A tryout. I don't
know what to do with myself. I don't know what to
write.
Thanks for the card. It got here at the right time and
saved me from a fate worse than

I was fine this morning. I was fine right through to the
afternoon, then on the bus coming home I got scared. I went
to Ellen's door and waited. I waited till I made myself knock.
The first stroke split the skin on one knuckle, but I screwed
my eyes shut and kept going. I am trying dammit. The house
was reeking of curried lamb. If she hadn't wished me happy
birthday I would have been fine. As it was she patted my arm
stiffly and said I'd be all right I said I know I said
I know.

I am TRYING dammit

So then I went to the SUPERMARKET where you can buy
EVERYTHING YOU NEED AND THEN SOME. I got a magazine
                        a tub of yogurt
                        gin
                                and I was waiting in the check-
out queue when I saw him staring in through the glass. I was
flustered and spilled the money and when I picked it up
again and went outside he was coming over

    Long time no see!
                            This thick moustache and
                            leather gloves

190

own practice out in Stirling
shire so just down to see the
folks

                                  so smooth skinned he might
                                  have plucked his chin with
                                  tweezers

she's fine thanks

                                  this burgundy coloured wool
                                  and tweed, no aftershave

and married now of course,
just waiting for her now
actually

                                  the same mouth but

                                      I couldn't remember his

So. What have you been doing with yourself lately? Still
dramatics is it?
We were at school together. I couldn't remember his name.
He scratched his nose: gold watch, roman figures.
Making a name for yourself I expect?
I said: I haven't been very well lately.
No, he said and smiled a sticky smile. No. Well. He
looked at the gold watch. Still engaged to that tall chap?
Paul Whatsit?
No I said. I haven't been too well.

He waved at someone behind my back and pulled his scarf
straight with both hands, then he walked away telling me to
Take Care.

A mirror spread out behind the space where he had been.
There was a woman in the frame, gawping, the fountain
bubbling up at her back. She was listening to a distant kiddy-
ride playing Scotland the Brave. Her coat was buttoned up
wrong so the collar didn't sit right, the boots scuffed and
parting from the sole. The hair needed washed and combed
and my eyes were purple. I looked like a crazy-woman/
wino/raddled old whore. I took another long look and went
into the chemists though it was closing and bought the

biggest bottle of paracetemol I could find. Impulse buy.
They had to open up the till again to let me pay.

Last minute, I said, smiling at the man working the keys.
I'm always last minute. You now how these things are.

I sip my drink.
Time is not a healer. I have a good memory. Razor-sharp.

gin in tissue
brown glass bottle of tablets
plastic tub of yogurt
birthday card
cookery book
magazine

Now I have some deciding to do.

It was too cold to walk back from the shops. I sat next to a
woman with a child, a little girl. The little girl stared with
these wide blue eyes, the head flopping heavily every time
the bus jolted the gears, slopping on the thin neck as though
it might break off and roll up the aisle. Chocolate smears on
either side of her mouth. The woman dabbed at her mouth
with a paper tissue then applied the tissue to the child:
mouth to mouth

a Dutch
a Germ

mouth to mouth/mother to child. They say you always
remember the taste of your own mother's spit on a handkerchief.

Look at the mess, she said, just look at you. I don't know
what I've raised. Sometimes I think they gave me the wrong
one.

Bitch.
An old man leaned over my shoulder with a curl of halitosis
whisky.

Bitches. Tell you one thing hen, one thing. Stay single.

The birthday card on the shelf falls over when I laugh. A
birthday card all the way across the Atlantic. Ellen's card

comes out of my pocket crushed. Someone took time out to find this for me and this is the kind of thing I do.

I can't decide what to do.
I used to spend a lot of time waiting. Women do. Women have this tendency to think things will be better if they wait longer
ie when
- I get away from my mother
- when I live with the man-I-love
- when I get away from the man-I-love
- when my mother loves me more
- anyone loves me more
- when I finish the diet/buy new clothes/get a haircut/buy new make-up/learn to be nicer/ sexier/more tolerant/turn into someone else

The thing is you can spend so much time in this fantasy future you miss what the hell is going on under your nose ie The Present. This Moment in Time. What passes for Now. I pulled out grey hairs and didn't notice my mother's because they'd always been there. When she got sick I didn't believe it. When she died I didn't want to know. She was most likely pretending to get attention, trying to make me feel guilty. Paul didn't talk. When I told him I loved him he got lines at the side of his mouth, wondering why I was trying to irritate him. The lines didn't go away as fast as they used to. David kissed me and the mouth was different to Paul's. David was ten years younger than me. Something clicked. Something just outwith the range of definition. I was getting older. I pulled out more hair and I left Paul.

I spent a lot of time spending time. Magazines told me to work on my awareness. I would wake up and think this is my One Shot at Today. I'm Young, Dynamic, Today's Woman. I'm Multi-Orgasmic. I have to Live Life to the Full. I didn't know what this meant but I thought it anyway. At the start of every day. It became pressing. I would get anxious if I hadn't done something new, discovered something, found a direction for my life. I filled in a diary I didn't

193

want to keep but thought I had to so I could record the
momentous changes that would occur now I was independ-
ent and free.
Today I
           walked to the beach on my own
           found out what you do with okra
           bought black nail polish
           planted leeks   etc etc etc. All strictly big
deals. I checked my eyes every night, searching for indelible
traces of ageing, read magazines on how to relax facial
muscles, keep my waist narrow, my bust firm. I flexed
vaginal muscles watching TV, practising my grip. Michael
was ten years older than me: grey at the temples. His jaw
trembled on a long kiss. We talked Sex/Love/How Many
Beans Make Five. That kind of talking had a logical conclusion of course. We reached it. The talking got less as the sex
got more. Phone calls in the middle of the night/ shared
looks and gestures/self-indulgent ironies: playing games.
Spectator sport before either of us

It was my birthday. He left late to go home. Paul came to see
me with a present while the sheets were still damp. I felt
confused and pleased Paul was there. Then the phone rang.
It was Michael. He said
    She knows.
Paul watched my face changing colour.
    Can I come tonight? I've nowhere else to go.

When he hung up I was sick.
Paul cleaned up the mess, crying because I was. When I
touched his hand he froze. Poor Paul. Big tears when I think
about Paul. I never anticipated a time when the telling of
love would just be hurtful. Jesus. Poor Paul.

Oh well.

Michael arrived that night with a plastic bag full of socks,
a change of jeans and nothing else. We finished the gin, a

194

bottle of plonk and the sherry. Next day we went gingerly round the cottage looking for space for his things, making shopping lists of food he wanted in my cupboards. Our cupboards. We made plans for his emancipation so he needn't feel he owed me anything. New woman, new man. No jealousies, no possessiveness, no demands. We filled in his housing form, arranged for days he could be alone. There was some stuff I hadn't expected from unexpected quarters. Maliciousness is unaccountable: you always assume people have better things to do. Once or twice I found myself yelling at kids in class over nothing, staring down the stairwell aimlessly when the bell rang. But I was coping, I was fine. Nobody needed to worry about me.

Then

My body knew he was dead before I did.
It shouted and yelled and punched the nurse who came with the needle, thumped its fists off the walls and screamed to try and wake up. My mouth promised whatever I did wrong I'd never do it again. But it's hard when you don't know what it is you did wrong in the

Dr Stead wanted me to be fully aware. I did too. I wanted to feel it all at once. I thought I had.

that feelin{
devant vu

Knowing too much at the same time as knowing nothing at all.
WRONG

I write a single word on the letter and look.

WRONG

It's important to write things down. The written word is important. The forms of the letters: significances between the loops and dashes. You scour them looking for the truth. I read *The Prophet*, Gide, Kafka and Ivor Cutler. *Gone with the Wind, Fat is a Feminist Issue*, Norman MacCaig and

Byron. *Lanark*, Muriel Spark, *How to cope with your Nerves/ Loneliness/ Anxiety*, Antonia White and Adrian Mole. *The Francis Gay Friendship Book* and James Kelman. ee cummings. *Unexplained Mysteries* and *Life after Death*. I read magazines, newspapers, billboards, government health warnings, advertising leaflets, saucebottles, cans of beans, Scottish Folk Tales and The Bible. They reveal glimpses of things just beyond the reach of understanding but never the whole truth. I fall into a recurring loop every morning after

The morning after

the courier's girlfriend took me through the woods to the shower block. I remember the terrible time just keeping upright with the hangover kind of thing when this man appeared suddenly on the road in front of us. A Dutchman or a German. I looked, remembered him by the poolside breathing into Michael's mouth. He must have been under the water for five minutes, madam. Madam. The same man this morning in another setting. And I smiled. I went into this set piece. I smiled and the man smiled back. We both knew we were doing something odd but neither of us could think what. We smiled at each other in a shaky kind of way and I couldn't move. The woman led me by the hand to keep me walking.

We went to the poolside and I looked into the water: the grout between the tiles, grey shapes like seagulls from the white surface. Like writing. At the funeral it was stifling and there was me up to the neck in black. I went to Spiritualist meetings, invoked the dead with incense, drank the scent from clothes and bottles. I read the tarot and said to godalmighty whatever it was I did wrong I'll never

Sometimes things get worse before they get better.

Sometimes they just get worse. Sometimes all that happens is passing time.

Dear Marianne,
I'm home for my first long weekend. A tryout. I don't know what to do with myself. I don't know what to write.
Thanks for the card. It got here at the right time and saved me from a fate worse than

WRONG

The gin starts to taste oily. I must be careful not to be sick in case I need a settled stomach. I made that mistake before. I need my stomach to be settled as long as I can manage. I want my decisions to be rational.

Christmas is coming.
The cottage melts under red spore dust less than two miles away. I have a magazine to read and two plastic bags of washing stinking of Foresthouse and distant vomit. The world needs to be set to rights. And I sit solidifying on this cold floor too lazy to get more clothes, looking over my shoulder to see who might be watching.

The other side of the Atlantic.

It is 2pm in the Blue Grass State. She will be working/teaching/plying the TV generation with books. Marianne trusts books. So do I. I imagine Marianne in the Bible Belt telling them about Burns and Shelley, laughing when they call her a Commie. Marianne is sociable and outgoing. She goes canoeing and camping out with good old boys, trades recipes with the womenfolk. She tours and sees piano players in shopping malls. Some nights she goes to Shoneys or Jackson's Restaurant for tacos, pizza and Rocky Road ice cream with her colleagues from Lincoln High: other nights, she goes home alone to TV dinners and repeats of I Love Lucy. She does these things with equal good grace. They will tell her about their marriage problems, wayward children and fantasy affairs. She invites confidence. Late, she sits out on the porch in shirtsleeves, enjoying the closeness of the night air, the scent of baking earth and magnolias. Writing letters.

But I'm trying as hard as I can dammit.
I'm trying as hard as

Other people. Other people interest me. How they manage.
There are several possibilities.

1. They are just as confused as me but they aren't letting
   on.
2. They don't know they don't know what the point is.
3. They don't understand they don't know what the point
   is.
4. They don't mind they don't know what the point is.
5. They don't even know there are any questions.

The first is too paranoid. Paranoia is a joke. I will not be a
joke. Rejected on the ground of unpalatability. The second
unlikely: it rests on the unpleasant assumption that other
people can't work out what I can work out. Since modesty
is a becoming trait in a woman, I reject the second. The third
is interesting and enviable but gets things no further forward. One can hardly *unknow* something, ie I am in no
position to alter the facts. The fifth makes me lonely and is
rejected on the same modesty clause as postulation 2 (see
above).
That leaves me with the fourth.

The difference is *minding*. I mind the resultant moral
dilemma of having no answers. I never forget the fucking
questions. They're always there, accusing me of having no
answers yet. If there are no answers there is no point: a terror
of absurdity. Logic will force me to do things where desire
hasn't a chance. Which leads us to
                    There is no point, ergo

It has possibly something to do with families therefore
possibly also my mother's fault. Maybe you could have
hereditary minding.

The Evidence:

1. My maternal grandmother died in a house fire. She laid out her marriage certificate, her teeth and glass eye in a row before she went to bed and left an electric fire burning in the corner of the room. The smoke filled the street. The coroner said it was an accident. She was eighty-one.

2. Aunt Connie took an overdose of painkillers. She had been refusing to eat for weeks and had hospital tests for some sort of brain-wasting disease. She left a note saying it was nobody's fault. She was sixty-eight.

3. My aunt Iris jumped over an iron parapet onto a railway track. Under the coat, they found she was wearing only an underskirt and her wedding ring. The family said they couldn't account for it. She was fifty-eight.

4. One of the cousins (I forget which) drove into a wall at fifty miles an hour. No-one was allowed to see the body. It was her forty-second birthday. No suspicious circumstances.

5. My mother walked into the sea. Not the first time she tried something like that but the most unusual one. It didn't kill her. She had time to come round and have four heart-attacks in hospital first. The wards were so busy, the bed was in the corridor on one visit. Hospitals don't have much patience with attempted suicides. Two days back home she had another attack and smashed her head when she fell on the fire surround. Six months after her sixty-sixth birthday. No suspicious circumstances.

The men are less interesting: coronary thromboses, bronchial disorders, mining accidents. Even some natural causes. With my father it was booze. That has possibilities.

I toy with suicide. I toy with pills, the fresh collection in my locker saved for emergencies. I toy with broken glass and razor blades, juggernauts and the tops of tall stairwells. I toy. But there's no real enthusiasm. My family have no real talent in that direction. Every time I try to work out how to do the thing properly it cheers me up. At least there's an escape clause if things get too much. This paradox can keep me entertained for hours till I think I'll go nuts. Joke.

Decision Time. Examine the facts.

I am twenty eight today.
Last year I was twenty seven.
This year things are different.

NEXT

The defendant is anxious, depressed, mildly paranoic and suffering from low self-image. Also guilty about all of these things and why not? The defendant refuses to see the Point or to accept what must be accepted whilst being fully apprised of the facts. She knows, ladies and gentlemen, yet the knowing and the knowing making a difference to the conduct is another matter entirely.

NEXT

You can't escape from the inside of your own head. You can't stop the runaway train/ the merry-go-round/ the speed of light/ the music/ the sun/ the tide and the sea. Or the snow for that matter. Nothing makes any difference to these things. They are all bigger than the individual.

NEXT

    Q.How many psychiatrists does it take to change a light bulb?
    A. One. But the lightbulb must really want to change.

This is of the essence. The defendant is afraid of health. There is a certain power in illness she is reluctant to relinquish for the precise reason it lets folk off the hook. People do not visit the unsick. The defendant's entirely selfish interest in the state of sickness is undisputed. Ergo

The logic of the thing is

the logic of the thing

the logic is

I turn off all the lights.

The switches under my fingertips.
The curtains are closed but with enough space apart to make
it possible to see in if someone is determined. Someone
might be. I think about music then change my mind. As large
a gin as the glass will take is fine. Then the paper bag. Cap
seals and cotton wool. The tablets flaking powdery stuff
over the palms of the hands. You're supposed to write
something. Touch of tradition. I chalk THANK YOU on the
painted floorboard with one of the tablets but it's indecipherable.

If you mean it, you do the thing with no escape clause. You
take them all. The whole bloody

Cheers.

It's my birthday.
I'm twenty-eight.
I'm freezing in this hellish livingroom.

What will I do while I'm lasting Marianne? What will I
do?

It gets colder

and someone taps
                    the window

It could be someone selling
  could be someone lost

                                        but
                                        it taps again.

There are no lights, no sign of my being home.
If I wait he will go away.

If I answer I have to accept what it says about me.
That I don't want to die. That I don't want to live very much
but I don't want to die.

It taps again.

My knees creak and buckle
forcing a run as the knocking comes again, louder. And my
hands choose, pulling the curtain aside to show breath
misting on the pane.

Through the cloud there is someone looking in, a white face
on an indigo ground. I don't have to focus. David holds a
bottle in one gloved hand. He mouths at the glass.

  Happy Birthday.

The line counts seconds.

        You sound happy. I never know what sort of mood
        you'll be in. What have you been

        have you been taking? Listen I need you to send

some stuff. Cheese. Cheese. Can you believe they've never heard of cheddar? maybe some oatcakes. Are you still there? Listen to me. Is that David? Let me talk to David, I want to talk to David. It's so good to hear you, not to have to say everything twice. They all make out they don't know what I'm saying over

are you still there?
It's so good to hear your voice.

The line blips and hiccups like a fish.
Marianne laughs.

ooo

David's gloves on the stair rail.

Ferns on the window. Through the fronds, a pink toy still there between the white weeds. I used to leave washing out there in all weathers, days on end. Once, the little girl from next door came up to the wire, squinting through to watch me. She kept up this chanting sort of thing - lady lady - while I was hanging up the stuff, shirts, pairs of jeans, things that didn't give away the fact I was alone, chanting and pressing something onto the mesh. When I got to the last shirt someone called her away so she just dropped the toy and ran. It fell on my side of the wire. Still there: this pink fish with blue fins surfacing between the jagged drifts. The only thing with any colour out there. Frost lends it a picturesque edge.

Saturday
The day after my birthday.
Christmas is coming.

I move through a house full of absent noise. The mug of tea
warm into my neck. Bits of torn tissue, empty glasses, record
sleeves, photos all over the shop. Shop shop shop christ. I
have to go to work. Tony will be there. A dozen or so half-
formed excuses and diversionary tactics could be gone into
but they merely mask the essential fact. I have to go. Tony
will be there and this is precisely why I have to go. I have to
look him in the eye. Look, people make mistakes. They
happen to everyone. You should be able to allow for
mistakes and know that's all they are. Just because last week
because he
just because

The trick is not to think. Just act dammit.
Act.

ooo

Tony smiles like melting butter as I walk up to the grille but
doesn't say much. We are all very busy or pretending to be.
Allan is full of the cold and miserable. Never mind, he says,
things can only get better. I raise an eyebrow and he smiles
through his hanky. He should know better. Once, he says,
he knew a man whose wife left him and his mother died in
the same day. A week later he had some kind of heart attack.
In hospital they found out he had diabetes as well. Allan
went to visit him in hospital, cheer him up. Never mind, he
said, things can only get better. That night, the guy's house
burned down. Since then Allan is cautious about philoso-
phy.

Tony breaks in when I laugh. We are forgetting where we
are. He tells me to come with him for cash slips. Allan is too

205

busy. I have to go. In the back room, he puts his arms round me and tries to push me against the wall. I look him in the eye but not long enough, slipping under his arm.

Don't, I say, shamefaced. A whisper. I don't even know if he hears me. When I make the tea he watches me from the other end of the space, biting chocolate.

Still too skinny, he says, sliding a hand out and onto my hip. When I push his hand away he tilts closer, offering the blunt end of the bar to my mouth. I'm brisk till pay time then run. Outside, I feel the notes in my hand and look down. An extra fiver.

Dear Joy,

I'm watching the Thanksgiving parade on TV at Heidi's. It's terrible. They have a replica of Olive Oyle 75 feet high. Outside it's raining just to complete the picture. Heidi is hysterical with delight: she loves Thanksgiving. She has already fed me cantaloupe with cheese, turkey with corn bread and cranberry sauce, two kinds of squash and three kinds of potato and fried okra. She sulked when I couldn't finish my pumpkin pie. Every time she bounces on the settee I think I'm going to be sick. I'm sure she means well.

Your present is coming.
                    Much Love Mxxxxx

Ellen laughs when she reads the card. We swap what we've been doing over the weekend. I tell her about David driving along the motorway, drinks out, sentimentalising where possible. Ellen likes a sentimental story, or appears to. I never know for sure. She invites me for Christmas and I say maybe, no promises. I sit till late watching the fire and the TV while she knits and she says to stay. She gives me Marianne's dressing gown and Marianne's slippers. I lie in Marianne's bed, the warm milk her mother made for me forming skin. When I am sure Ellen is asleep I go out onto the landing and pour the tepid milk down the sink. Space and the big house cracking its joints. The window at the top of the landing makes the sky go into next week, the week after that. This big house on the top of this hill. Look ma, No Hands. Three bathrooms for christsake. At night it cools down to a chill.

> Decisions must be faced rather than put off any longer. You can't wait to leave things behind, go on a spending spree perhaps, fly to exotic destinations. But can your pocket take the strain? Think things through then think again before doing anything this month. Things can be enjoyed in moderation!

The models look funny. When I check the front I know why. It's typical of Marianne to have a nine-year-old magazine under the bed. Her mirror glints when I turn over. Lumps under the rose-pattern duvet. The lumps move when I do. I wonder what time it is in Kentucky, if Marianne is awake too. I watch Marianne's mirror for the rest of the night, moving occasionally. I'm still there.

ooo

T E S CO's is full of red and green crackers, hanging baskets of walnuts and almonds, tiny pitted clementines, Christmas cacti, plastic greenery. I root among the apples, pears and onions, oranges and lemons, leftover autumn marrow, checking the list I made from Ellen's cookery books. Dried fruits, peel, three kinds of sugars and malted vinegar. Cloves and nutmeg. In danger of being driven to excess by the individual plum puddings and doggy-treat stockings. De Luxe crackers for christsake. MAKE THIS YOUR BEST EVER CHRISTMAS! Every front cover says the same thing.

The phone rings unanswered while I spend the afternoon slicing pieces out of my fingers and grating my nails. Pared lemons sting the grazes and drip onto the lino. Shetland fishermen on the radio. Sugar seeping with juice like flooded sand. Some onion and apple are left over, two overripe tomatoes. The onions give me heartburn.

The Lovers, inverted.
The World.
The Hermit.
Fortitude. The second of the four virtues.
I can only guess.

The phone rings late.

PHONE [Man's voice. Mid-Atlantic drawl] Hi. I knew you'd still be up.
ME Who is this? Who am I speaking to?
PHONE Cmon, guess. Can't you guess? It's me.
ME No I can't guess. Who is this? David?
PHONE Who the hell is David? [The voice changes tone sharply] No it's not bloody David. It's Tony.
ME [Relief it isn't a random weirdo] Of course it is. Hello Tony. So.
TONY Hello. I should think so. David. Who is this David?
ME Just a friend. Ex-pupil. What do you want?
TONY [Smooth again] How are you feeling this lovely night?
ME [Irritated] OK. Look why are you phoning? It's after twelve.
TONY Hell, that's not late. The night is young. You sound a bit funny. Did I get you out of bed?
ME [Pointed] Yes.
TONY No problem. What are you wearing?
ME Look, Tony, what is it you want?
TONY Nothing, nothing. Whoa there. No need to be anxious. Just wanted to hear your voice/ know how you were/ what you were doing this fine night/ if I could come over. I'm only a mile or so down the road, a call box. Won't take me a minute to get over.
ME [Spelling it out] But I'm in bed, Tony. I'm tired.
TONY You won't be tired once I get there. I've got a bottle

	of champage and your birthday present. Something pretty for a pretty lady.
ME	Look. Tony. I am tired. I'm going back to bed.
TONY	All the better. Look just leave the door off the catch and slip upstairs. You'll hardly notice me arrive.
ME	[Tentative] Have you been drinking?
TONY	A little. [Manly giggle] Just enough to make me think of you. I'd love to see you in this bracelet. Let me come round and you can try it on eh?
ME	Tony I'm tired. No.
TONY	[Pause] What did you say?
ME	[Trying it out again.] No.
TONY	What do you mean, NO? NO? Don't play up. Just do it. I'll be round in less than a minute.
ME	NO. I mean it. I'm going to bed and I'm going to sleep. I'll see you in the shop. Stop calling me.
TONY	What do you mean fucking no? Stop mucking about.
ME	I mean NO, Tony.
TONY	Look just do it OK?
ME	No. I'm going to hang up if you don't stop this.
TONY	[Pause] Look just
ME	I mean it.
TONY	OK OK. I can take a hint. [Sound of feathers ruffling]
ME	I'll see you in the shop next week, OK? (Pause) OK?

The line purrs.

Sticky feet across the kitchen lino. I make tea in the dark, guessing the level for the cup. From the outside I am too visible with the light on. I don't know where he was phoning from. I check the locks and windows just in case. Twelve lids lie gold with streetlight in a row beside the cooling marmalade.

The twisty road leads ahead to a thick wood.
Something hides in the wood: I hear it breathing.
The road falls away behind us like shed ribbon
under the full moon. There is no way back.

He holds my hand as we look across the fence and
into the field. I know someone is buried here but he
must never know, must never find out. His profile,
the curl of hair on his collar. In the moonlight his
teeth are unnaturally long, his eyes bright. The grip
of his fingers hurts. Someone is buried under the
earth of this purple field. I'm the only one who
knows. Michael's fingers grip tighter and my arm is
numb.
I'm afraid he suspects what I know.

My neck is numb too.
Soon the sun will rise over the edge of the hill and it
will be too late to speak. My mouth won't be able to
open. The sky stains with pink. I want to speak to
Michael but I'm suddenly not sure it's really him at
all. If he's really there.

Something wet spills over my empty hands. He isn't

His distant back melts
into the woods.

ooo

There's no milk. Only a packet of biscuits going soft,
making everything in the cupboard foosty. I pour black tea
and put on the immerser just as something scuffles in the
porch. Barelegged in an outsize shirt, I almost drop the cup.
My eyes are bloodshot, my hair greasy and my toenails are
chipped. And there's someone at the door. Please god make
it not a man.

The scuffle comes again and the door hurls open. I stand
helpless on the rug in a giant shirt and watch
Paul.
Paul scuttling
backwards
through the door
with a box in his arms.
Tall and thin and too good to be true. The advance of Paul
across the rug. That he's seen me looking this awful before
is no reassurance.

This came for you, he says and dumps the box on the
floor.
His face gives nothing away. A tag with my handwriting on
the handle, my handwriting clearly labelling the address.
Perfectly normal handwriting. Paul shows me the side of the
box burst and taped again: stamped with DOVER PORT
AUTHORITY. It wasn't his fault the box got burst. DOVER PORT
AUTHORITY take all the blame.
I smile bravely.
Thanks for bringing it round.
It's the sort of thing you say to a delivery man/ policeman/
meals on wheels. He doesn't notice or doesn't point it out.
Don't mention it. Listen. He checks his watch. I have to
rush.
Och surely you have time for a coffee or something. I'll
make it fresh. I sound like an advert but he accepts.
As long as it's quick then. Just one.

He doesn't follow me into the kitchen. I know he doesn't
want to be in a confined space with me and feel bad. The
sound of his feet on bare boards is embarrassing. The house
is a mess. There's nothing to eat but soft biscuits and
chutney, day-old marmalade.

Maybe better not.
His voice comes through the wall.
Oh? I haven't enough throat to shout loud and he doesn't
hear me properly so he doesn't know if I've heard him. He
has to come to the kitchen door to say it again. We are closer
together like this. Our voices lower, almost whispers. It

makes us sound kinder.

Better not after all, thanks. He shrugs. Best manners.

Oh? I say. Eyelid scratching the surface of the eyeball, a heaviness between the lashes like sleep crust that makes me want to sleep. Lie down where I am and

No, he says. Should be getting back. Busy.

Oh. I don't know what else to say.

We say Well simultaneously. Oops. Embarrassed smiles. I'm running out of time.

So how are things with you? I say.

Fine. Fine. He manages to look cool, polite. How are you?

I manage. I manage.

We move and breathe with exaggerated quietness, as though listening for something far away.

Listen, do you want me to carry that stuff upstairs for you? It's stuff from Spain. Um. I can wait while you unpack it if you like.

I say No, it's OK. I'll manage.

Sure? You'll be OK? Sure?

Yes, yes. Sure. I'm fine. I want to tell him the truth. It's only my things. Brought all his home with me at the time. Just my things.

Oh, he says.

He looks at the lino.

I figure if I say nothing maybe he'll open up. I'm wrong. He turns and looks meaningfully at the door.

Better be going then.

Just one coffee?

No really, better not.

Yet he hangs loosely at the door without moving. Every time I see Paul it's like this: full of things unsaid. I'm supposed to guess. If I talk straight he gets flustered and runs away. I don't know what he

I never see you these days, I say.

He looks as though I've hit him. We go into a stiffer mode altogether.

EXLOVER   No. I'm...uhh...Busy a lot. [Long pause]

212

HARRIDAN	So. You're off then.
EX	Yup. [Tosses keys nonchalantly in one hand]
HARRIDAN	Well. [Pause. Someone shouts YOOHOO outside the window. EX takes sharp inbreath. HARRIDAN driven over edge of discretion] Can I ask you something? I never know what you don't want me to say. Can I just ask you something? [Thinks about the times they said they'd always be friends and how hopeful it seemed then. Can't understand the difference.]
EX	[Feigned puzzlement] Sure. Sure. [Thinks about the times they said they'd always be friends and how naive they were then. Can't understand why she can't understand.] Anything you like.
HARRIDAN	[Bull by the horns] Are you all right? Are you happy?
EX	[Considers for a second. Tries to look calm while brain is in overdrive and eyes glaze over] I Happy enough.
HARRIDAN	[Spitting out more] I keep wondering how you are. You hardly ever come. Am I doing wrong things? Give me clues. Do you want me to pretend not to be..I don't know. What is it you want me to be?
EX	[Sighing] No No It's not that.
HARRIDAN	I can't talk to you any more. I'm scared you want that to be the case. Can I touch you? [Sensation of breaking glass] I just want to touch your arm. I get the feeling I'm not going to see you again.
EX	[Blushes and looks at floor] Don't be silly. You'll see me. [Both know now this isn't true but no-one is allowed to say it out loud. They have to play out the charade to the end. Anything else would be tacky.]
HARRIDAN	[Waxwork] Yes. So, what's your new place like?
EX	Just what I've been looking for. Great. You'd like it.
HARRIDAN	I liked the old place. You didn't tell me what day you were moving. I would have liked to see it again.

EX   Didn't think.
HARRIDAN No. [Meaningful pause. Is scared face cracks]
EX   Well then.

[The kettle whines and switches itself off in another room. They're at the front door now: his backing away and her pursuit]

HARRIDAN [Herculean effort] I hear congratulations are in order. [Sickly smile goes in place and locks. It won't shift]
EX   What? [Flushing to the roots. Tears hole in rug with tip of shoe] Oops. Look what I did. Oops.
HARRIDAN Don't I get to congratulate you? [Smile gets even bigger. Clasps his hand. It is surprisingly warm and receptive.]
EX   Yeah. Sure.
HARRIDAN No date set?
EX   No. Not yet. Um. [Eyes cast around room for something diverting. There isn't anything] Look I have to go. The van's waiting. I brought your mum's chair. The one you said you wanted from the flat. I brought it. I'll go and bring it in.
HARRIDAN [Almost yelling but smile getting in the way] Fine.

[Pause. Neither of the two move. He freezes with his back to her, blocking the doorway: she stares at the floor.]

          Tell me you're happy.
EX   [Stops dead in the doorway. Keeps his back to her throughout] I'm getting married.
HARRIDAN Yes.
EX   I know what I'm doing. I'm all right.
HARRIDAN Good. [Knows is telling terrible lie] I just wanted to be sure.
EX   Joy. [Pause] You're gonny have to stop this. You don't need to worry about me any more.[Goes out]

214

The ice-cream van pulls up outside playing Raindrops Keep
Falling on my Head. I wait at the foot of the stairs while Paul
struggles back in with my mother's wicker chair.
  Where will I put this? he says, not able to see.
  Anywhere. It doesn't matter.
He drops it to one side of the rug and there's hardly enough
room.
  Be happy, I say. I hope you're both happy.
I hear him sniff but keep my eyes on the floor.

The box he has left behind. The wicker chair.
The sound of the van jarring into wrong gears and out again,
coughing away into somewhere else: past the end of the
street, the main road, the motorway and godknows. Swimming costumes and towels, clothes, a phrasebook.

Screaming would be good. But I never scream. I can write it
down but never do it, never actually. Do it. The fist limply
into the yellow wall: soft plaster pressing on the side of my
hand then hard, miniature rockfalls scuttling like rats
inside. My forehead against the plaster leaves a stain. There
is no-one here and the house is full of noise. No-one would
know if I were to, if I were just to open my mouth and. Just
yell. Lungs working, the singing rising in my throat, the
pulse in my temples. The moaning noise I make when I'm on
my

only me and
          what was his name

so I scream dammit.

I scream

There is cold.
Giggles from next door.
Pain in the joints, boredom of stillness.
You can't stay too long in one place. Something base and human as the need to pee. The body converts and processes. It does what it can.

I will Take Advice and Try Harder.
Persistence is the Only Thing that Works.
The More Something Hurts, The More it can Teach Me.

The hospital expects me at four thirty. Four hours.

ooo

Brushes and screwdrivers clink as I reach with the key. The door isn't as sticky as you'd think after all this time. But all the newspapers: big pile of unsolicited stuff right behind the door. I don't know how you stop these things coming.

I shut myself in, go through to hollow dampness and pepper: mushroom smells. The cottage turning into a salad.

Colour co-ordinates. The curtains still match the wallpaper but dirtier. The windows haven't been opened for months. I pull a book from the case I painted white, skimming the pages to see the worst. The mildew and the creeping damp, mould and decay. The armchair is cold to the bone. An old newspaper folds on itself in the rack and the telephone cable trails along the wall.

HOME SWEET HOME

A dishcloth over the fireplace. I trace the outlines with my finger. Present from Marianne the day I moved in. A joke. We sat in the bath drinking wine and tore down all the wallpaper.

The radio is in the overnight bag. Some music before I open the door on that hall and whatever else is down there by this time. The first channel plays Golden Oldies. Blue Suede Shoes as loud as it'll go without distorting. Elvis is coming with me.

I turn the handle. Look inside.

Paprika puffs around the toe of my shoe. Further in, the louvres of the cupboard doors are silted, the same brick-coloured powder on the skirting. And there's something on the bathroom lintel, moving.

A flat-headed toadstool, wet beads glittering in the ruffle underside because it's so dark in here. I swear it swivels when it hears me coming. Inside my pocket, past the ribbons of tissue and gum wrappers, the hard shape of the handle finds my hand. Elvis is politely aggressive in the livingroom. The screwdriver tip catches the edge of my pocket and slides out. My hand rises level with the mushroom cap. I watch the shaft sink easily into the soft head, turning with a faint clicking sound. The fungus slithers so far down the length of metal then heaves and drops, twisting once on the carpet before it lies still. Kitchen mushrooms hide near the skirting and above the jamb. They are safe today but not much longer. I leave the screwdriver on the carpet and turn. Elvis swings straight into Hound Dog.

The bedroom door is fine but the rest is sliding. Wallpaper coming off and billowing up in the middle of the sheets. I tear two strips completely to the skirting no bother, deliberately make a mess. The clothes in the wardrobe smell like wet dogs. I pick up his dressing gown and wrap up the hammer and the rest of the tools. The dried flowers and ornaments, the bedside books are coated. Letters on top of the wardrobe curl in a rubber band.

Elvis is all done by the time I'm done. I switch off the disco stuff and leave by the back door to circle to the bus stop, the place where people outside used to look in at my house. On the other side of the road, the newsagent puts up boards for the afternoon. He scales a ladder holding the boards, trusting his feet. He waves across, wondering where he's seen me before.

What's more, I wave back.

ooo

Four roads converge from the surrounding fields. Forest-house sits at the top of the hills. You can see it for miles. It comes into the wide wrap of the driver's window as I stand hunched on the platform.
   Visitors is it? Somebody sick?
The conductress is chatty. I say Yes, somebody sick.
   Somebody close? I say No. Just a friend.
She doesn't take my fare.

The rush of nausea takes me by surprise. I breathe deep and take in the dry air and sickly pine of the corridor as though it is something new. Veins popping on my cheeks after outside. These stairs go on forever.

Ros pronounces her Rs like Ls all the way through her chop suey, slanting her eyes. Really she's depressed. Bramwell isn't coming tonight. Maybe he's tired of her.
   Bramwell? I say. Bramwell?
All this time and I never knew her boyfriend's name.

   Yoohoo.
Sean bursts into the dayroom like the sun. A pot plant waves up above the level of the brick-thick dayroom fog, yellow chrysanthemums. I drop my knitting and see the needles

bouncing on the carpet, the row of old women bobbing like a row of heads on the water.

Yoohoo.

Mrs Morrison waves back at Sean. Is that your man, pet?

I tell her no, it's somebody else's.

When we're alone I don't know what to talk about and fuss with the flowers. I ask for jokes. He likes telling jokes: never very good ones but I want to hear Sean telling me jokes. I ask him how many psychiatrists it takes to change a lightbulb and he knows.

I watch him laughing and hold the plant tight.

Later I don't feel the pills going down.

I don't feel anything at all.

ooo

Nancy comes bright and early for OT, her last session before she is Mrs March. We can still call her Nancy, though. Today we go downstairs to make party invitations in the print shop. Janey and Phil collect inky letters and slot them into wooden racks. They have been here before. Nancy knows exactly what I'm for.

You're the teacher so you'll be good with spelling. You stay there and check the spelling when they put the letters in.

Phil tells me he was no good at English at school. He was no good at anything at school.

I wait while they arrange things and can't figure anything out. Everything is backwards and upside down. I assume it's all right but don't have a clue. Nancy thinks I am being difficult.

John takes the block and chooses buff card. Nancy tuts.

Not that colour. That's all wrong for the time of year. Don't you think? I think so anyway. Red's best but we've no red. Red for Santa. Christmas invitations, see? But there's no red. People come in here and just lift things. There was plenty of red last week. Use pink. It's closest. Use the pink.

They're not for a stag night are they?

John starts production with the pink. One of the letters is backwards but nobody cares. Janey and Phil start another block. Kathy won't do anything and gets huffy. Nancy tells her she's lazy and Kathy tells Nancy she's a Big Cow. Everybody turns and looks. John sniggers nervously then stops. There's a horrible minute where there's no noise at all then Nancy shouts. She has had enough. Ee-nuff. Thank god she's getting married in a few weeks. Her lip trembles. And not one of us had the decency to give her a card.

Janey talks non-stop on the way upstairs knowing that's what she's doing. Side-effect of something she's trying out. If it doesn't work she'll be for the electric. 1D are running a stall at Christmas, for supplies. Mina's in charge. That's what's up with Nancy's face. Janey wouldn't be surprised if she sabotaged the rag-doll knitters and the bathsalts committee for OT sessions out of spite. OT sessions never make anything for the Christmas stall. There's your proof. We never do anything useful in OT. We never even do anything nice.

Nassim tags along under the pretence of moving us out but really to join in. He likes a chat with the girls. Ros comes and sits on Isa's bed: they giggle like girls behind the bikesheds. Isa is new.

Ros says, Never mind about Christmas Fayre. Guess what.

She's going home for Christmas. We coo like pigeons and Isa hands round Black Magic. I hover over the box knowing not to take one would be bad form. I steel myself for the dipped brazil. Without warning, Janey wheels, pushing her face too close.

You don't like us do you?

I just look. I don't know what else to do.

Think you're better than this place, don't you. Think you're better than me. Eh? Well fuck you teacher. Fuck You.

220

I will Take Advice and Try Harder.
Persistence is the Only Thing that Works.
The More Something Hurts, the More it can Teach Me.

Repeat twice after meals.

It's OK to have Bad Days.
You Can't Make Other People Love You Into Existence.
Everything Worth Having is Hard as Nails.

I talk to myself for ages and don't care.

OOO

MAKE THIS YOUR B E S T E V E R C H R I S T M A S!
The hospital is full of magazines. They all say the same
things.
MAKE THIS YOUR B E S T E V E R C H R I S T M A S!

Present suggestions for the man in my life, games the
children will love, recipes for my BEST EVER CAKE, tips to help
me carve goose (try a change this year). New ways to wrap
those special gifts, how to make the big day stress-free,
pretty tree ornaments that will last and last to become
family heirlooms to treasure. A feast of television fun is
coming my way. I learn Winter-warming favourites, store-
cupboards musts for party punch, the sleekest hair news,
after-dark tricks for sultry eyes, the lips everyone will want
to catch beneath the mistletoe, what my choice of cards says,
whether I'll last the pace.

Dear Kathy,
Please help me. Every time I think about the
coming holiday I am filled with dread. I retired
earlier this year, shortly after the marriage of my
youngest daughter. Living alone (I am divorced)
suited me well for a time. But the thought of
Christmas and New Year is making me

Dear Kathy,
I am a single parent and unemployed. This is not
something I usually dwell on overmuch, manag-
ing to take the rough (and there is a fair amount)
with the smooth. But Christmas time is specially
difficult. My ex-husband demands to see the kids
and is able to buy them

KATHY WRITES

Oh dear, how fraught a Happy Christmas can be: and that's
just a sample from my postbag! Let's stop and look at the
thing more deeply. Look at the whole essence of the season
of goodwill. For that is what it is. And it's all too easily lost
among the commercial excesses on television and the high
street. The best way to get more out of your Christmastide
is fill it again with that sense of giving in the truest sense.
Why not spend Christmas day by paying a visit to a local
home or hospital? You needn't take anything: just your time
and a willing smile. Often, a child's demand for a large
present is merely a way of demanding something from you
they feel they're not getting the rest of the year. More
attention, perhaps, or time with you just for fun. Get them
involved: making things for the tree, singing carols together,
walking in the snow is free and will give more real pleasure
than any soon-to-be-broken (and all too often expensive)
toy. How about little home-made surprises in a pretty
stocking, a letter from Santa? A small token given with love,
even a sincere hug and kiss, are worth more - and obviously
so - to those around you. Check out our make and bake
pages for ideas. Thinking of others. That's the real trick
behind the Merriest Christmas!

This is your birthday month so look alive to the
changes that are surely on the horizon. It will
have its share of surprises, not all of them pleasant, but all challenging. Submit to chaos for
once!

I want to be ready for the surprises.

222

I have to learn to submit to terrifying chaos and not revert.

> Dear Kathy,
> My cheeseplant (healthy until a few months ago)
> is turning orange and wilting for no apparent

WHAT BECOMES OF THE BROKEN-HEARTED? Stories to make your heart beat faster for Christmas.

I have to stop reading these fucking magazines.

> *I dream*
> *a white bench, cold metal against the base of my spine. We do not touch. I am uneasy. Engine sound comes through the soles of my shoes and the sea churns behind the walls.*
>
> *His voice is hollow overhead.*
> *He has to go now. He will try to see me again soon but there's no telling when it will be. His wife is somewhere on board. Touch is a risk.*
> *But I'm scared I will never see you again: what happens if I never see you again?*
> *He says Shhh, one finger to his lips. Shhh.*
> *My head fills with bursting bubbles.*

> *Something terrible has happened.*
> *I can't think what it is.*

> *I reach for his hand and he is no longer there. In the distance his back melting between crowds of anonymous others. I shout and he stops. He turns slowly.*

His mouth is a wide 0, eyes open to the sky.
No-one else sees and I realise he isn't there at all. I
am entirely alone on this ship, churning on through
foreign water. The sound of the engine fills my ears.

OOO

Isa cries. She's lost her relaxation tape.

It's OK to have Bad Days.
All in its Own Good Time means Slowly.
Everything Worth Having is Hard as Nails.

I tell Isa and she listens. Nassim barges into the therapy
session in a bad mood. There's someone to see me and I'm
never anywhere sensible. Don't I like to have visitors? We
should think ourselves lucky. He hates it here.
I'm sorry, I say. I'm sorry about this terrible job.
He tells me not to be cheeky.

Frank waits looking shy at the end of the corridor in a
leather jacket and Rupert scarf. I never saw him look shy
before. He hands me a box of chocolates before he speaks.
I got the letter he says. What is it you want to talk about?
I say, Something and nothing. What's school like? and he
says, You know, just how it always is.

The coffee machine starts clattering in the corridor, shedding teaspoons. I've been waiting for Frank to come but
now he's here it's hard to start. I know nothing about him:
just chance meetings in the staffroom.
Look, he says, do we have to talk about work. It's bloody

boring.

This is a big help. I smile and say No. Just you talk to me. Anything you like.

What kind of thing? he says, and looks up.

Other things. I know. Travel.

Out of the blue. But when I say it I know it's the right thing. It would be good to travel. Frank is Polish so I figure maybe he knows about travelling. What you do to travel is just go, he says. Simple. Just do it. To hell with whether you've got the money. I laugh and he says he knows where I can start the travelling. Sean has a promotion and there's a do at work.

Travel to that, he says. Start big. No really. You should come.

I look at him hard in case it's supposed to be funny.

I mean it, he says. Come. Just to prove you're not cuckoo. Half of them probably think you're in a strait-jacket most of the time. They just don't know. Come and talk to people.

I'll think about it.

No, he says, don't think about it. Come. Just do it.

On the way out he stops, looks round.

I'm surprised though. All this.

All what?

This. This place and everything. When I got the note from here. I'd never have figured. I thought you had more fight than that.

I think about it after he's away.

Maybe there's less to me than a lot of people think.

I dream we're somewhere falling apart.

Michael whispers not to tell anyone our secret. He is only pretending. We can meet every so often in this derelict building but I must not tell. The man touches my arm but doesn't look like Michael. When I look hard, I see he has someone else's mouth. I ask when will I be able to die too and he laughs. It is part of the joke. I must always wake up from these dreams and know he's really dead after all. He keeps laughing while he speaks. It's all part of the joke.

ooo

A card from Marianne with a stick-on turkey for my locker.
   Don't let the Turkeys get you Down.
I keep the card and give the turkey to Isa. She needs it more than me.

Dr Two turns up on time but I don't smile.
 So, he says, how are you?
 I pause and say, How are *you?*
He won't play. He asks me again how I am.
 How do I look?
He tells me I look fine. I say, In that case I feel fine/I feel OK/ I feel as well as can be expected. I don't smile.
 How did the long weekend go?
 I say, Fine/ OK/ as well as can be expected.
He suspects a joke.
 I say, Yes it's a joke but he's still on edge.
 So how are you really?
I say fine/ OK/ as well as can be expected. Really and truly. Then I smile. Just teasing. That's all he was waiting for.

226

One more long weekend he thinks, then out for
Christmas. What do I think?
I give all the right responses.

ooo

Dear Marianne,
Your present arrived this morning. I know you
probably bought it for me to wear here but I'm not
going to. It would end up smelling of hospital.
Anyway, a red dressing gown is asking for trouble
in here, this near Christmas.

I'm going to a party in a fortnight. Sean is being pro-
moted. I promise not to roll my eyes, drool or eat
with my fingers. I can think of other things that are
more original. David isn't sure it's a good idea but
I have to start doing things on my own. It may as well
be now. Also Psychiatric are having a carol concert
next week. I enclose a ticket. They gave me ten to sell
and I couldn't think of anyone who'd buy one. I will
have to return nine but I am donating mince pies
instead. I can make them in OT. I wrote to everyone
who came to see me and told them I'd be at home
most of the time from now on. I haven't OK'd this
but I have made up my mind. And I told the agency
to sell the cottage. I don't know if I am making good
decisions or right decisions. I am just making decisions. That is one step further forward. I am trying
not to mind about making mistakes.

PS Your mother has invited me for Christmas. She will try
to feed me till I burst. HELP.

I write *love*. I sign.

227

ooo

Nine envelopes behind the door.
A late birthday card from Sam, five Christmas cards. One
wrong address. DOVER PORT AUTHORITY monopolises the rug.
I scramble round the edges to the kitchen, shedding envelopes.

1. An appointment with an estate agent on Monday.
2. A disclaimer from the holiday insurance people, stubs of
   tickets, a taxi receipt.

The phone rings and it's David, wanting to know how I am.
He's studying for exams and won't be able to come till
Sunday. I say Of course. Great. Come when you can then.
   Oh?
He isn't sure about the tone. I laugh, little-girl stuff: still
breaking this laugh in.
   Yes I say. I'm fine. You don't need to worry about me.
I know, he says. I know.
Just as he's about to hang up I make myself say it.
   Listen you don't need to visit that place any more. I could
be out soon. Thanks for ...Just thanks.
And hang up fast. He'll think I'm crazy.

Outside, a huge white cat walks along the tops of the railing
stubs, paws careful on the slats, tail as straight as balloon
string. Half-way he stops and looks down. No chance. He
faces the front and just keeps going.

Mhairi arrives dead on time. Paint in her hair and behind her
nails.
   Maybe I should have cleaned up, she says. New headstone etc.
She can say the oddest things. Neither of us wants coffee. We
get in the car and drive for miles.

The cemetery is in an open valley, the hills on every side

dotted with houselights and cows. It's halflight when we get there and we can't see the animals too clearly. We hear them moving around. The houselights fall in rows. We have to go past umpteen rows to get to the new green. First in a fresh plot. He was here alone for a while: now there are four more. The headstone is white with black letters, just the name and the dates. Start and finish: both quantities known.

I count it out. Nine years between us now: my birthday makes the distance shorter. This also means one day, I will overtake. The squares of turf are still visible but healing over. I think about him being under there but feel nothing much. Over my head, cloud gathering: rolling dustballs into one dirty corner of the sky. I forgot to bring gloves. A whippy wind catches some of Mhairi's flowers and blows them over the grass, single stems of Old Maid's Lace. She chases and gathers them back together, weights them with a stone. We walk together past the slabs of marble, chittering. I'm here and Michael isn't. I want to get out of the cold.

ooo

Sam is leaning on the front door, waiting when we get back. Just finished his exams. Mhairi gets animated and says we should go for a drink. She never goes to pubs but this is different. Sam follows on the bike. She doesn't know anywhere to go so we end up somewhere strange. Early Friday evening. The place is full of men celebrating weekends and office parties, leather jackets and open-necked shirts, dressed to kill. Occasional women in corners rearranging their cleavage, flashes of jewellery through the fug. Happy Hour: we can get a Pina Colada or a Midori Smoothie cheap. Midori Smoothie. We have to yell over this disco mix out the juke-box: just the one drink and no more. Something ordinary for godsake. Mhairi makes a face at her half of lager. She isn't comfortable here either. I bolt the gin, try not to scan as though I was looking for the door which I am. Then something catches my eye through the smoke, something familiar near the chrome railings round the

counter.
Norma Fisher.

Shivering, feeling my eyes over her skin.
The centres of her eyes are red under the lights, knowing
something is out of place though she can't see what. She's
wearing black too: thinner and a new hairstyle. Holding the
bulb of the glass as though she's trying to shatter it with the
one hand. Someone shouts in her ear and the head dips, eyes
still casting for the source of the footsteps over her grave.
Fixed as a rabbit in the headlights. Was this how she heard
when I telephoned, the box at Heathrow, waiting for the
Glasgow connection and yelling to make her hear. She
didn't hang up then. But now I have no bargaining power.
I realise for the first time I'm afraid of Norma Fisher, that
she may well be afraid of me.

Mhairi nudges my arm.
Her drink is finished and she wants to leave. Sam thumps his
empty glass down as the record stops, into the fraught space
of people knowing they are talking too loud and trying not
to care. And Norma turns.
Our eyes kiss and break.
Nothing more.
There's no point. Norma Fisher cannot love me into existence either. I have to let her alone. Sam tries to take my arm
but I push him away and walk out alone, heels dead in the
thick pink pile.
Head up, up. Just do it. Act.

Sam runs me home.
We hang around at the door, not able to work out how I can
kiss him goodnight through the helmet. I squeeze his hand
instead. The hand is all gauntlet. He pulls away raising the
visor and puckering his lips like a catfish. He likes to see me
laugh.

*The night before he died we went walking along the
sea.
The way back went past the edge of a wood, a rim
of bushes. Look, he said. Look. Lights coming and
going.
Fireflies.
Beads on luminous thread.*

*We came back to sit by the poolside, looking out,
drinking. Someone was swimming, slicing effort-
lessly like a shark into the tight black skin of the
water. He said You're very quiet and I shrugged.
There was nothing to say.*

*Cheap brandy in glass hammocks. We looked out
over the pool, the white arms of the swimmer rising
and sinking out there in front of us, just visible in the
dark.*

*The tent under the trees.
We lay together not touching because of the heat. In
the morning we made love and I cried. Not an
everyday occurrence but it happened sometimes.
Then we washed at the tap, got ready for the pool.
I carried a paperback and three kinds of sun cream.
Careful, watching out for the other burning. His
semen welled inside me as I rolled on the towel. His
mouth touched my neck then the shadow length-
ened, moved into the sun.*

I'm going to swim.

The footsteps measured as he walked away.

ooo

Steam.
The bathroom full of smoke. I soak up to my neck then scour
the skin raw, rinse and wash my hair. Twice. With a pair of
dressmaking scissors I face the mirror and cut my hair short.
Spiky. I colour it purple with permanent dye I bought ages
ago and never used. While the colour sets I use the scissors
to cut short my nails. I tint my eyebrows black. Tomorrow
I will have my ears pierced, twice on one side. It will scare
the hell out of David.

Allan shouts Tony though I tell him not to. I hear the shop
working without me on the other end of the line, someone
jingling change as they wait outside. The box is freezing.
Tony clicks his watch off the receiver and coughs. He
sounds concerned.
    Allan tells me you're not coming in today, Are you OK?
Is everything all right?
I tell him I'm fine and not to worry. Just one of these things.
He wants to know if I'm coming in next week, they really
need me next week. I tell him to count on me and he sounds
relieved. He stays on the line for a while, coughing. I have
to hang up first.

A pyre of clothes on the kitchen floor.
I immerse them in the sink in small loads, scattering washing
powder. My hands get sore but I keep washing. I wash all
day: grating the cloth against itself, twisting the fibres
together, freeing the stink of Foresthouse. I use washing
powder and cologne and wash everything twice till my
hands look cooked and my fingers wither. Look. The skin
of my wrists is transparent, like cellophane. You can see the
arteries underneath. I hang the clean clothes outside in the
frosty air to freshen. The pink plastic fish is still there among
the long grass and litter. It squeaks when I lift and push it
back through to the other side.

232

DOVER PORT AUTHORITY splits easily down the middle. Smells of trees and suntan oil, aftershave, musty cloth. The things are only dimly recognisable: a polka-dot skirt, patterned tee-shirts, thin little slices of underwear and some trashy books. I make another pyre of everything except the sunglasses and a shirt then have second thoughts about one of the tee-shirts. Everything else, back inside the burst cardboard, a neat packet. The scent of it makes me dizzy when I walk to the binstore. Nothing to do with me any more.

I change bedlinen and sweep the floorboards. I shake out the rugs. I reach high with the brush for the cobweb strings in corners and pull down the curtains. I wash all the windows and wipe them down with newspaper to make them clear. It gets late before I realise and I have to run.

Just five minutes.

The receptionist is suspicious but Dr Stead makes time to see me. Just five minutes. I tell him how I will be getting out of hospital soon and he looks as if to say it's fair enough. He thought it was a mistake but perhaps not. He says he doesn't mind being proved wrong. When I ask how he is he says he's emigrating. They know how to treat doctors in New Zealand and the climate is better. I tell him I'm sure he's right. He gets embarrassed at the two jars of marmalade but I don't care.

The shops are full of white-frosted cakes and mince pies with bits of plastic holly. Turnip and tangerines. I buy a bottle of whisky (seasonal) and see tree lights carefully piled at the checkout. Cheap. Little fairy lights with glitter frost. I read an article about depression that said buying yourself presents is a good thing: break the routine and spoil yourself a little. The little boy in the trolley in front watches my indecision, slathering his mouth with melting Mars Bar. I check the price again and think what the hell.

ooo

The heating clanks uncertainly. The whole house throbs.
These floorboards are terrible. Maybe I should bring a rug
from the cottage or something, keep in the heat. Just now I
have the whisky.

The whisky. The tree lights. Wee diversions. I find a glass
before I let myself sit then open the presents in the correct
order. First things first. The box for the lights sifts tinsel stuff
down the front of my jeans and onto the carpet. Very festive.
I have to take the plug off the turntable to try them out
though. Sip of whisky then stand back. They work first time.
Pretty pinks and greens, yellow and blue, glitter on the
shades making sparks. I turn to the window and see the
house interior ghosted on the black outside: the yellow walls
boiling with colour.

No radio.
Takes a minute to remember I left it at the cottage, near the
hallway door. It'll be dark over there. All that peeled-back
paper hanging from the bedroom walls. I can always clean
the worst of the visible damage, strip and wash the walls,
open the doors to let winter air refresh. I can leave all the
windows open as well: there's nothing anyone would come
in and steal. I can paint the window frames white again, lift
the carpet tile in the hall with a scarf over my nose and
mouth. I'll make lists. Things that need to be done for the
next week or so. The week after that.

After that.

Tomorrow.
David will come. I may visit Ellen.

But tonight I have no radio.

I find the Walkman and riffle tapes. Wee bit of Debussy. I
lock it into place, fit the headphones. The battery light

bleeds. A clicking in the ears as breath escapes in a white curl. Cold enough to snow. I could get the duvet maybe. Later. Tree lights throw colours on the wall and whisky washes wide in my chest as
the music comes through.

The lights and this sound.

Maybe

Maybe I could learn to swim.

Another mouthful, picturing the sea. Casting out long arms into the still water. I am naked, hair long as a fin down the pale spine ridge, flexible as a fish, the white profile against black waves, rising for air.

A little light fiction.

Shadows in the corner of the room give me away. I'm gawky, not a natural swimmer. But I can read up a little, take advice. I read somewhere the trick is to keep breathing, make out it's not unnatural at all. They say it comes with practice.

I take another mouthful of whisky, slide my finger on the volume control. Waves rippling through the headphones. And something else.
The human voice. I listen watching the coloured lights, fanning like sea anemones over the ceiling, till the music stops.
A click and tape whirring into silence at the end of the reel.

The voice is still there.
    I forgive you.
I hear it quite distinctly, my own voice in the empty house.
    I forgive you.

Nobody needs to know I said it. Nobody needs to know.

The tape winds on into empty space. Inside the headphones I hear the rise and fall, the surf beating in my lungs. Reach for the bottle. Watch the lights.

THE HISTORY OF VINTAGE

The famous American publisher Alfred A. Knopf (1892–1984) founded Vintage Books in the United States in 1954 as a paperback home for the authors published by his company. Vintage was launched in the United Kingdom in 1990 and works independently from the American imprint although both are part of the international publishing group, Random House.

Vintage in the United Kingdom was initially created to publish paperback editions of books bought by the prestigious literary hardback imprints in the Random House Group such as Jonathan Cape, Chatto & Windus, Hutchinson and later William Heinemann, Secker & Warburg and The Harvill Press. There are many Booker and Nobel Prize-winning authors on the Vintage list and the imprint publishes a huge variety of fiction and non-fiction. Over the years Vintage has expanded and the list now includes great authors of the past – who are published under the Vintage Classics imprint – as well as many of the most influential authors of the present. In 2012 Vintage Children's Classics was launched to include the much-loved authors of our youth.

For a full list of the books Vintage publishes,
please visit our website
www.vintage-books.co.uk

For book details and other information about the classic
authors we publish, please visit the Vintage Classics website
www.vintage-classics.info

penguin.co.uk/vintage